N

S

Sandy Stream

Grant Brook

Lean-to

Rip Dam

Busta's Cabin

Big Mouse Inn

Ray's House

To Milkraket

Prologue

Well, how do I start? A friend of mine got married at the Big Moose Inn. Later, after all the ceremonies had ended, I found myself at the bar talking to the barmaid and I asked her if she knew anything about the stuffed bear head that was out in the lobby. "No," she had said. It was there when she started working at the Inn 15 years before. She asked one of the cooks and a waitress but no one knew anything.

So, I told her, I would tell her the story of the Hoof-ma-goof and Johnny Blueberry. I ordered another drink and began the story.

His story was told to me when I was just a boy of ten or eleven. Twelve to sixteen boys, two teachers, and maybe a couple of parents for chaperones. We spent the night here at the Big Moose Inn before it changed for the season.

Chapters

Chapter One
The Man from Away

I asked her if she had ever heard of Johnny Blueberry, knowing if she had never heard of the Hoof-ma-goof she would not have heard of the man he killed. She said no so I explained that a bear had killed him and that's why he was on the wall. And so, the story begins.

Johnny Blueberry was a logger by trade. One of the men that worked the river with pole and pick. He had his leg broken badly. Not being able to move as quick as he might need to, his time on the river was done. He had to figure out a way to make money. By the time his leg had healed enough to get around, the wild blueberries were out so Johnny started picking and people were buying.

Men working on the river didn't have time to pick blueberries but Johnny did. He would sell them to the people in town and to the cooks at the logging camps. Everyone started calling him Johnny Blueberry.

"What does that have to do with the bear?" asked the barmaid.

"Just a little background on Johnny," I told her.

"I thought this story was about the bear," she said.

"The Hoof-ma-goof," I replied.

"The what?" she asked with a funny look on her face.

"The Hoof-ma-goof," I repeated. "It means three-legged bear."

"The bear only had three legs?" she questioned.

"When it was shot yes," I answered.

"You see there was a man from away. A flatlander, a trapper wannabe, that didn't have any business being in the Maine woods. He thought he was going to make it big up here trapping fur but the Big Maine Woods would prove to be a little more than he could handle.

The flatlander rubbed people wrong right from the start, bragging about all the things he had seen and done. Few people believed his tall tales. He could see he would have to prove himself to the locals. He started to build a cabin off by himself. It was on the north shore of Millinocket Lake just south of Grant Brook. This was late spring. It was a one room cabin about twelve feet wide and sixteen feet long, just right. The little pot belly stove would have no trouble keeping it warm even in the cold of winter. There was a bed in the back, a table up front, and a sink by the stove. He also put in one small window so he could see the lake.

Few people would stop by but Johnny would when he was out fishing on the lake. He would row his twelve-foot wooden boat out in all kinds of weather. "Fish are wet and still feed so I can be wet and still catch 'em" he would say when people asked him why he would fish in the rain. When he had good luck and caught more, he would stop by and check on the flatlander.

Well I know the flatlander trapper wanna be had a name, but for the life of me I can't remember it. I'm sure it isn't the only thing I have forgotten over the years about this story but it seems no one else remembers any of it at all. So, for this story, or my version of it, I will call him Busta.

"How you making out Busta?" Johnny asked as he landed his boat. "Got some fish here for ya if you want."

"Yessa. I'd take any you want to give. I haven't had much lunch and besides that I need to put some up for stink bait this fall."

"You need to get you some eel. They make the best bait and it lasts the longest in the woods," Johnny told him.

"Eel? Well, heard of them but never caught any. What do you use for bait to catch 'em?" Busta asked with that odd look on his face.

"Well we could use the guts of these here perch. We can have these for suppa and catch some after dark," Johnny explained.

So, Johnny showed Busta how-to put-up eel for bait. He told him how to make a set that the locals use. He said he had spotted new beaver and otter signs up on Grant Brook and that he might try for some martin further over by Sandy Stream.

"I thought this was a story about the bear," said the barmaid.

"It is," I told her. "But I didn't say it was a short one. May I have another drink, and may I continue?"

"Yes, please do," she replied.

Well it went on like that for most of the summer with Johnny stopping by and giving Busta a hand. When fall came Johnny moved in to town. With his messed-up leg the snowy winters made it hard for him to get around. Summertime camping was one thing, but winter in a tent? Nope, not even with a good stove. Johnny stopped by before leaving the lake making sure Busta had enough wood for the winter. Traps were boiled, stretches made, and the bait had just the right stink. Fall was in full force with cold, crisp mornings and leaves of all different colors.

Busta was ready for trapping. He ran his line like he and Johnny had talked about. Up Grant Brook after the beaver dam, then heading across the ridge towards Sandy Stream. It would be a good hike, seven and a half to eight and a half miles round trip. With the canoe ride back to camp it would make a good day out. Busta got all his gear ready and loaded it in to the canoe the night before he finally made his first run.

Chapter Two
The Line

Up he was long before the sun, food in his belly and ready to go. Out to the canoe he went. There was a cold chill in the air and a mist on the water. Busta paddled up the lake to Grant Brook. He set a couple traps on the point where the brook met the lake. With any luck he would catch a coon or maybe an otter. Up the stream a ways four more traps were set. There was a nice big beaver dam there and he figured that would be a good spot. Busta then loaded up his woven backpack filled with big traps, little traps and the stinky bait. He would stop on the edge of each ridge and make a set. Mostly simple cubbies, a few sticks and a good tree with a "Y" at the base. Then Busta would take a piece of fur and pour some of the stink bait on it and hang it in a tree nearby. Whether the wind blew up or down the ridge he figured anything in the area would smell it and come to investigate. Where the hard wood ridge met the cedar swamps traps were set for marten and fisher. Built on a leaning pole with a trap placed below the bait would do the trick.

Busta had been out all day and got so carried away with setting traps he didn't realize how far away from his cabin he was and what time it was until the sun dropped down in the sky. Standing on the ridge Busta overlooked the lake. He was miles from his canoe and his nice warm cabin, but he did know of a lean-to not far away. That's where he would have to spend the night on his first day out trapping. With his back to the setting sun he headed over two more ridges where the two little ponds were hidden. A lean-to and a fire pit was there just the way he was told. An axe and wool blanket were the only items there but that was all Busta needed. He got a fire going right quick then worked to get enough wood for the night. Once he thought he had enough he stopped to relax.

He stripped down to his union suit, (one-piece long johns with the back-trap door for you younger folk that don't know) to dry out. Walking all that way you can work up a sweat! Busta was wet up to his elbows and from the knees down from tripping while crossing a small brook.

He stood there thinking about the day and the sets he had made. Which way to head tomorrow he kept thinking as he fed the fire another log. He had two options. One was to head down to the lake and set traps along the shore for other coon and fox. Or he could go back over the ridge to where his last set was made and make a big loop. One ridge over to the north, then following the top of the ridge west, then south to the brook, this would bring him to where his canoe was. Busta thought he could get some marten and fisher up on the ridge. Maybe even a bobcat. He had some traps left but only a few so he would only set in the prime location and fill in the other good spots later if he found any on his trip.

Busta got all his clothes dried out and hung them in the back of the lean to. They didn't smell too good. He had spilled a little of that stink bait on his hands then wiped it on his pants without thinking. Not a good move. Boots on sticks by the fire helped them to dry out good. Busta went over everything he had left with him as his clothes dried. Traps, food, and bait. He got everything ready for his trip back. He tried on his pack. A lot lighter he thought and figured he could make good time so he would take the big loop.

A few more logs on the fire then he bedded down. Curling up in the thick wool blanket in the little lean-to with a good fire going he would be fine for the night.

At first light Busta was up and ready to go. He was in too much of a hurry to restock the pile of wood he had burned. He just made sure the fire was out then put the wool blanket back on the wall of the lean-to where he found it. Busta put on his pack and headed out, driving the axe in the tree next to the wood pile as he passed up over the ridge to his last set.

A coon was sitting there waiting for him when he finally reached it. Nice, he thought. Busta remade the set, then tied the coon on top of his pack. Today he thought his load would just keep getting lighter but even with the coon on top he would make the big loop.

Down in the valley and back up on the next ridge he went. Busta was going to be picky today so he passed up making a set in the valley even though he thought he should. Marking the spot he found with a cut to a spruce tree, he kept moving. Up on the ridge he found the 'horseback'. Busta would follow this back to his canoe. Every time he dropped down in to a saddle or a draw, (a dip in the ridge) he would make a set.

Busta kept marking his trail with his hatchet. A little missing bark on a three- or four-inch tree stands out, but for the most part it was just the lay of the land that showed him which way to go. Ridge to ridge, horse back to saddle to brook. Simple, he thought, as long as he didn't miss the left on the ridge.

After making a dozen sets or so, Busta finally made it back to his canoe worn out and wet and smelling like stink bait. He loaded the canoe with his pack then started the trip back down the stream. He checked his traps that he had set the day before. One rat and a mink he would add to his catch. Busta thought that wasn't bad for his first time out and all.

Back at the cabin, he couldn't rest. He unloaded the canoe, got the fire started, then began taking care of the coon that would be on the menu for suppa tonight. He got them all skinned out and quartered up. In the pot with a little salt the coon would sit while he took care of the other animals. The muskrat was quick but taking care of the mink would take a little more time. Cutting or nicking the hide would cost him money. With the fur on the stretcher, he cleaned up the rest of the mess. He would use the rat on the next trip out as bait so he put it in a pail with the parts of the coon he didn't want to eat. There was a big hemlock tree on the other side of the outhouse that had blown over and uprooted. Busta figured this would be a good place to throw all the scraps that he wasn't using for bait. That's where he tossed the mink and what was left of the coon.

Still smelling like that stink bait, Busta stripped down outside and hung up his clothes. He washed up a little then got to eating suppa. A potato on a rod inside the stove would cook it up quick. A well-seasoned cast iron pan and a little salt pork would cook up the back straps and hind legs of the coon. Busta added a half an onion in to round out the meat.

While he sat at the table he thought about the last couple of days. He wondered how many more traps to bring and why he didn't replace the wood at the lean-to. That kept bugging him knowing he would need to use it again. He should have taken the time. Busta laid everything out for his next trip before loading the stove and laying in his warm, cozy bed. Far better than the floor of the lean-to.

First thing in the morning Busta loaded the canoe and started up the lake to Grant Brook. Nothing on the first two traps. When he got to the beaver dam though he had a 'rat' in one trap and a good size beaver in another. The other two were empty. Resetting the traps but not wasting any time, Busta got ready for his hike to the lean-to.

The muskrat would skin out quick so Busta took care of it and made another set not far off in the woods using the carcass of the rat for bait. After making the set he grabbed the beaver and tied a rope to its tail. Finding just the right tree, one with a good short limb, Busta hung the beaver ten feet off the ground. He would take care of this back at camp.

Up over the ridge he went, pack on his back, following the trail he had walked and made two days before. Nothing at the first two sets so when Busta hit the draw between the ridges he made two more sets. A cubby would be the first one at the base of a hemlock. A few small limbs on the side and some tips off the hemlock branch to cover the top would make it complete. He used the muskrat from two days before for the bait and topped it off with some stink.

Next Busta saw a leaning tree about eight inches across wedged between two trees. It was a perfect place to put some of that 'coon'. With a stick across the tree just above the wedge and a #2 Victor to guard the bait, he went off over the ridge to check the final set which was the one he had caught the coon in. As he got closer, he could see a trap hanging from the tree. Nice, he thought, but only for a minute. The closer he got the more he couldn't understand what he was looking at. Busta finally made it to the set and could see it was a martin, but only part of one. Its front foot was securely held in the trap. Something had eaten it right out of the trap. Busta couldn't figure out what would do this. Coyote he thought. That's all it could be. But to leave nothing? Maybe bobcat? No sign though and to leave just the feet was odd. He had never heard of anything like this. So, he remade the set just like before. Where you see one pine martin you usually find more.

Busta added a #2 long spring under the tree where the martin was hanging. He covered it with just a few leaves. He figured whatever did this would be back. Coyote, bobcat...the #2 would be waiting.

Off he went to the last set of the day. The trap was sprung but nothing was in it and the bait was gone. Now Busta was thinking just a coincidence, nothing to worry about. He remade the set and went off to the lean-to. He wanted to get there and put up some wood before it got dark. Busta had made good time even after stopping and making the new sets and remaking the ones that were tripped.

When he got to the lean-to things didn't look right. Someone or something had been there. The stump he used for a seat was tipped over and the forked sticks that he dried his boots on were no longer sticking out of the ground next to the fire ring. Some of the rocks were moved and rolled away. Then Busta noticed the wool blanket. It was no longer hanging on the back wall. Out on the ground next to what was left of the wood pile, it lay torn and covered in dirt and debris. He took off his pack and walked over. Picking it up and shaking off the leaves and sticks, he was mighty glad he had brought another from home. The wool blanket was still usable, just dirty with a few holes in it. Busta stood there looking around. What a mess. This was the work of a black bear he thought. After looking around he found some proof. It was a bear. Tracks in the ashes of the fire ring were unmistakable. Five inches across the pad of the front foot. Good sized bear Busta was thinking...but where are you now?

No time to waste. Night was coming soon. He started to get as much wood as he could before darkness set in. He would clean up around camp by campfire light. A couple nice big blown down trees

11

were handy and made for easy work. In no time Busta had replaced the wood he had used the night before and had enough to get him through the night.

With fire going Busta replaced the forked poles to dry his boots and the rocks that circled the pit, all the while keeping his rifle handy. Busta was a little nervous and uneasy. He wouldn't be sleeping good tonight. After a while he settled down and curled up in his wool blanket with the other wrapped around it. Busta laid down with rifle in hand and a good pile of wood burning. He figured he could get some sleep.

It seemed like he had just closed his eyes when he heard a pop. Pop. Pop. Pop. Busta opened his eyes. He didn't move, just laid there listening. Pop. Pop. His hand closed on the grip of the rifle. Pop. Pop. There it was again! What was it? Busta had never heard the sound of a black bear smacking its jaw. The popping made its way around the camp just out of sight. He thought he could hear some heavy breathing but wasn't sure. This was all new to the flatlander from away. The popping went away suddenly. It was there, and then gone. Busta faded off to sleep listening intently for what he couldn't see.

A raven welcomed the sun with a "caw, caw!" Busta jumped. He was surprised he was asleep. Looking around trying to figure out what just woke him up. "Caw, caw!" The raven was just above the lean-to and Busta jumped again. "Get out of here you damn bird!" he yelled. He took a deep breath. He was glad it was just a crow and not a bear that woke him.He got up and took the ripped wool blanket and put it back on the wall of the lean-to hoping it would still be there when he returned.

Back to the wood pile he went. He wouldn't leave it shy again. Since the blow downs were handy, he would do a little extra before heading out. With plenty of wood on the pile and the fire out, he got his pack together and headed out.

When he reached the first set that he had remade the night before Busta got mad. Bait gone, set trashed and trap sprung...with nothing in it! A quarter to a half mile away from the lean-to, Busta didn't think it was the bear but he was thinking, ok, I'm not out here feeding animals. I need to do something different. Busta remade the set about a hundred yards away but he still used the same stink bait and lure. He thought that would matter. Off down the trail he went and up over the ridge, stopping at each set to add lure and check bait. All the way back to the canoe without anything except missing bait. Busta was happy to see the beaver still hanging up in the tree and even more happy to see an even bigger beaver in a trap sitting on the dam.

After taking care of this beaver and cutting the one down from the tree he loaded up the canoe and on down the brook he made his way. The water on the lake was rough and the sun was getting low. Warm wind coming up from the south was making the normally calm side of the lake hazardous. White caps pounded against the canoe. Busta kept paddling for camp, grateful for the second beaver. It helped hold the front of the canoe down. In the heavy wind he worked hard to make it back to camp.

Once back at camp Busta unloaded the canoe. He put the pack on the porch and the beavers on the skinning table. He got a fire going in the stove then grabbed his knife and started on the beaver. Like the 'coon' before, this would be suppa. Beaver is quite tasty if done right. He would have his alongside some potatoes and wild mushrooms that he had found up on the ridge. After skinning and hooping, (stretching the skin by lacing it to a small hemlock tree bent and tied in to a hoop) both beavers he took the back legs and back straps in to the house. In the pot with half a cup of salt he'd let this rest a while.

Now back outside he needed to take care of the rest of the beavers. Taking off the front legs for bait, he set them aside. The rest Busta carried over to that big uprooted tree. He tossed them down and threw a couple spades of gravel over the top covering most of them. He made sure the canoe was tied up for the night then went down and took care of the pack and his blanket. Busta cooked everything up. He would take some with him on his trip back to the lean-to. As he sat eating, he thought about that popping noise and the bear tracks. He hoped he was just passing through and that he wouldn't lose any more fur. Busta settled down for the night.

When he woke in the morning the rain was coming down and the wind was whipping. He decided it wouldn't hurt any to let the trap line sit. He went outside and flipped over the canoe. Back in the house he would work the beaver a little more, scraping and tightening the lacing to help stretch it just a little more.

He decided to make a nice stew to help ward off the chill of the rain. With the fire going strong and the soup pot on the stove Busta cut up the beaver he had cooked the night before and added it to the water along with a nice big potato and a good-sized onion. He went over to his stack of goods. A carrot or two would be a nice addition to the stew he thought.

The next morning Busta woke early. He packed his backpack and loaded it in to the canoe before light. He made himself a biscuit with butter for breakfast then off up to the lake he went. The wind was calm and the temperature was warm. It looked like winter was going to be late. The south wind that blew in the storm was leaving a nice day behind.

Busta reached the mouth of the brook at sunrise. He didn't expect anything in the traps on the point but the animals were on the move in the storm. He had another mink in a pocket set. On the opposite side of the stream a coon sat looking at him as he landed the canoe. This was a good way to start the day he thought. Busta loaded the coon in to the canoe and remade the set. A little of that stink bait and some lure would refresh the set after all that rain. Up the brook Busta paddled to the beaver dam. Nothing in the traps but there were bear tracks on the landing. Really? he thought. It couldn't possibly be the same bear.

He took the coon and the mink and hung them in the tree where he had hung the beaver a couple days before then headed into the woods. Up the ridge he went. Busta's worst fears were confirmed. With each set he passed the traps were sprung and the bait was gone. Even when it looked like he had caught something there wasn't anything in the trap. Just a little fur of different colors. Busta was determined to get more fur so he remade each set putting more bait and lure on each one all the way back to the lean-to.

With all the rain Busta had a hard time getting a fire going even with the semi dry wood he had put in the back of the lean-to. A lot of birch bark and some dead spruce branches helped him to finally got it started then he went to have a look around.

15

More bear tracks everywhere. The bear had spent some time there that was certain. Busta wouldn't be sleeping well tonight.

He loaded up the fire with a teepee style pile of wood. This would give off a lot lighter and help the damp wood to burn better. One or two pieces of wood at a time throughout the night kept it going.

Out of the corner of his eye Busta thought he saw a shadow move. He got up and added more wood then he thought he saw it again. Busta went for his rifle. He knew that if it was the bear messing with his traps, he wouldn't get to keep any fur until the bear began its hibernation. It would be a welcome addition to his meat catch back at camp.

Boom! Busta jumped and spun around. The bear had slammed the back of his lean-to. Popping his jaws, the bear disappeared into the blackness of the woods. Busta started yelling, "Get out of here you damn bear! And stay away from my damn traps!" Crash, crash! The bear hadn't left he was just staying out in the dark moving through the shadow of the fire. The bear kept circling the camp and popping its jaw, jumping Busta every time. Then out of nowhere, through the smoke, Busta saw the bear. It was standing on its hind legs out in the shadows just watching. Busta blinked and rubbed his eyes thinking it must all just be in his head. As he came to realize it was the bear, he hurried to take a shot. Just as he pulled the trigger the bear disappeared. He heard the bear balling and crashing through the woods. "Got 'em" Busta said. He marked the ground so he would remember where the bear was standing in the morning. No one follows a bear at night, wounded or not.

Busta loaded more, a lot more, wood on to the fire. He didn't want any more surprises tonight.

Wrapped in his wool blanket with his back against the wall, he could barely feel the heat of the fire but this is where he was going to spend the night. With rifle in hand, Busta closed his eyes.

Boom! Something slammed against the back of the lean-to right behind Busta. He jumped up and almost fell back, stumbling all the way to the fire. Hammer back on the rifle and scared almost to the point of shaking, he grabbed more wood to add to the fire. Busta circled the fire the rest of the night.

The sun cracked the horizon and Busta is relieved that the darkness of night is gone. Now that he could see he began to investigate what had got him so shaken a few hours before. Gun in hand with hammer back, Busta slowly looked behind the lean-to. A big branch had fallen off the hemlock tree. It hit the ground tips first sending the broken end slamming against the back of the lean-to. Busta felt like a fool. Scared of a damn tree he said to himself. As he grabbed the branch it dawned on him that it happened twice last night and only one tree had fallen. No tracks would be seen with all the pine needles on the ground. Busta started to drag the branch out of the fire. He stopped dead in his tracks and looked at the back of the wall. There were four fresh claw marks a half inch deep at eyeball height in the old logs. Busta knew he was on the other side of the wall when the bear had made the marks. He dragged the branch to the woodpile then walked over to where he had marked the ground so he could figure out where the bear had been standing. About twenty-five yards he thought, right by that big pine.

Busta walked over and surveyed the ground. He found the overturned and shuffled leaves on the ground where the bear had turned to run away but no hair or blood did, he find. "I couldn't have missed," he said. "He was standing right there. How could you miss?" Busta kept looking, following the tracks that he could find. Losing the tracks not far from camp, he kept working the ridge looking for some sign. Nothing was found and he was going the wrong way. He still had to check the rest of the lines so he headed back to the lean-to. Busta loaded up his pack and off he went.

Up over the ridge he found the last set he had tended. It was just the way he had left it. Happy the bear had not returned to it, and with no time to lose, Busta headed off for the rest of the line. Thinking he was running late, Busta kept up a steady pace. One set after another the same thing as before, bait gone, traps set off. He knew that this bear was going to be a problem.

When he got back to the beaver dam, he dropped his pack next to the canoe then he went to where he had hung his coon and mink. But Busta didn't like what he found. The rope was chewed through, coon gone and mink destroyed. Busta was mad. He took off back into the woods up his trail just to see. Yup. Just what he thought. His first set on the ridge was destroyed. The bait was gone, the trap set off and the set needed to be remade but he hadn't brought anything with him. He turned and headed back to the canoe. When he got to it though, his pack wasn't where he had left it. He knew he had left it next to the canoe but now it was on the wood line next to the trail. Busta grabbed it and threw it into the canoe. He jumped in and pulled off for the lake. Just before he rounded the corner, he looked over his shoulder only to see a bear standing at the spot where his canoe had just been.

Busta kept paddling for the lake. Rounding the point out on to the lake he looked over at his sets but never missed a stroke. Nothing in them and no need to stop. Just need to get to camp. He would be safe there. He never thought when he turned around again just to look back at the brook that the bear would be there. Even though Busta was far from the point, he could still see the bear pacing around on it.

Reaching camp, Busta put the canoe up then took his pack up to the house and made sure he had enough wood in the cabin for the night. Tomorrow he would head for Millinocket. Busta needed help.

Chapter Three
The Trap

That night Busta didn't sleep well again. Every time he dozed off he would jump and wake back up. Even though he was safe in his bed he thought that he could hear that bear outside popping his jaw. In his cabin with four walls, not three like the lean-to, he thought he would be able to have a good night sleep. But not tonight.

The next morning Busta launched the canoe. He paddled down to the dike to start the long walk in to town. He hoped he would be able to hitch a ride from someone working on the dam or a logger heading in to town. It wasn't long before Busta got a ride. A supply truck was heading to town to restock. "Need a lift?" the driver asked.

"Sure do. Name's Busta."

"I'm Paul," said the driver.

Busta asked how the dam was coming and the men made small talk.

"So, you're not a logger. What brings you up here?" Paul asked.

"Trapping fur," Busta answered.

Paul laughed. "Fur? How you making out?"

"Not so good," said Busta. "Was doing okay but now I have a problem."

"Really, what would that be?" Paul wasn't ready for Busta's answer.

"I've got a bear problem. It's following my line and eating my bait and destroying my sets. It stalked my campsite the night before. I took a shot at him and thought I hit him but never found anything. Then on my way out of the woods I see him two more times following me down the Grant Brook. I couldn't get a shot because I was in the canoe and he was over my shoulder when I was looking back."

"Wow. That's quite a story. Never heard of a bear doing that," Paul said, thinking Busta was telling a tall tale. "So, what are you going to do now?"

"Not sure but someone in town must have an idea. I was thinking someone might have a bear trap that I could buy," Busta replied.

"Don't know about that but the Millinocket Foundry could make one I'm sure."

"Thanks for the information and the ride." Busta got out of the truck and wondered where his friend Johnny might be. He would head down to the center of town. Busta figured most people would know Johnny so he started asking around. He found Johnny working on the dairy farm out by the railroad station.

"Busta, how's the trapping? And what are you doing in town? I didn't think I'd see you 'til winter was in full roar," Johnny said.

"I've got a problem," Busta explained. He told Johnny the same story he had told the truck driver. "I don't know what to do."

Johnny told him he didn't know anyone with a bear trap, but the truck driver was right. The foundry could make one any size he wanted. Busta thanked Johnny and off he went. The foundry was not far, just on the other side of the station. Busta started walking to the office sign. When he reached the foundry, "Can I help you?" a man asked from an open doorway. Busta turned to see a tall, slim man covered in soot.

"Ya," Busta said. "I'm looking to have something made."

"What might that be?" The man held out his hand. "I'm Pete."

"Pete, nice to meet you. I was told you guys could make anything here."

"Yup. We can do just about anything. What do you need?"

"A bear trap," Busta said looking Pete straight in the face. "I have a bear that needs to go."

Pete could see Busta was serious. "Come on in and we'll talk Your pack will be safe out here," he said.

Busta reached into his pack and pulled out one of his beaver traps. A number four long spring with teeth. Then he followed Pete in to the shop.

"Now what you got going on?" asked Pete. Busta sat the trap down in front of Pete.

"Can you make this with a twelve-inch jaw spread?"

"Ya," said Pete, "But why?" Busta started to tell Pete what was going on. After he finished Pete looked at Busta and said, "Ok then. Let's see what we can do. How long you in town for?"

"As long as it takes," Busta said. "I'm not going to catch anything with that bear walking my trap line so there's no reason to head back to camp without it and the lake is a long walk away."

"You have a place to stay here in town?" Pete asked.

"No," Busta answered. "Didn't think that far ahead."

"Well why don't you hang out here for a while. You know anything about steel? You know how to use a torch or forge?"

"No," Busta said, almost ashamed. "But I'm not afraid of work or to learn what you guys do here."

"Well we have a couple guys out sick and if you're willing to work we might be able to help each other out. Sound good?"

"Yes sir," Busta said happily. He had no idea how much this trap was going to cost or how he was going to pay for it. "What's first?"

"Well, I'll introduce you to Bob. He'll walk you through everything." They walked over to the next building. "Hey Bob!" Pete yelled. Bob came out from around a big piece of equipment. A stocky man in his forties, covered in soot just like Pete. It was clear to Busta that these men put themselves into their work.

"This man is going to help out today. Put him to work. Start with the coal shed while you get metal to make one of these." Pete handed Bob the trap that Busta had brought. "But you need to make it bigger. This here is Busta. He'll give you the details. Alright?"

"Ok boss," Busta said.

"Busta is it? Come with me. What we going after with this?"

Busta told Bob all about the bear. Bob listened but didn't believe everything he heard. Bob took Busta up to the coal shed.

"There are two bins down that chute. Shovel is in the corner. Both need to be full. Stairs are behind that door. Come find me when you are done. Any questions?" Bob asked. Busta shook his head no and Bob walked away. Busta walked over to the door and went down the stairs to see how much coal he would have to shovel. At the bottom of the stairs he found the forge. This is where they melted steel and poured it into molds. Beside the steps were two pins made of steel with removable fronts. The front of the bins had boards that could be removed as the coal was shoveled out. It was a good thing he had gone downstairs. All the boards were off on one and three off the other. Busta found all the missing boards and stacked them in the slots completing the front of the bins. Back upstairs he started shoveling the coal. A couple hours had passed when Bob came up to see how Busta was making out.

"How are you doing Busta?" Bob asked through the dust in the air. "Looks like you've been working hard." Busta's face was covered in black dust. "Let's go check out downstairs." Bob was impressed. "Nice job. Looks like you're done here." Both bins were over-full. The coal had started to back up the shute. If Bob hadn't shown up when he did Busta might not have stopped until he saw coal at the top of the shute.

Back up the stairs and out the door, Bob walked Busta down to the building where Pete had introduced them. They walked over to a table. Busta was thinking, now what, sweep the shop or some other laborious job. Busta stood at the table. His trap sat in front of him. A few pieces of metal strips lay around the trap.

"What's next?" Busta asked. Bob looked at Busta.

"Now we put this thing together," he said smiling. "How big you need the jaws?"

"Well the track I see was at least six inches across and that was the front. So, twelve inches or so; give him a little room."

"We're going to put teeth on this thing, right?" Bob asked.

"Oh. Yes, if we can."

Bob grabbed one of the pieces of the metal. He locked it in a vice and started cutting down the middle with a torch. When he got a little way down he started to zig zag making big triangular teeth. A little trim on the ends and it was ready. Bob took it over to another piece of equipment. He slid the piece of metal between the rollers and pushed a button. As the rollers turn, the thin strip of steel rolled into an arch. One more time through and it was a nice half circle.

"There are your jaws. What do you think, big enough?" Bob asked.

"Wow," Busta said. "Yeah, that should work. It should hold him."

"Ok. Now for the springs," Bob said laying the jaws back on the table. He picked up two of the other pieces from the table. "This is what we are going to use but we will need to use some heat. Let's head back to the forge."

Bob laid the two pieces of steel in the glowing red coal. With a few puffs of the bellows the steel started to turn a glowing orange red. Grabbing a two-foot pair of pliers. Bob pulled out one of the pieces of steel. Laying it on the anvil, he folded it almost in half. He did the same with the other piece. "Let's go grind these up," Bob said to Busta who was impressed at the ease that Bob worked the piece of steel in to a spring. "I'm going to let you grind these smooth okay? Just look at your trap. If you have any questions just ask. I'm going to cut out the rest of the pieces."

"Oh ok," Busta said. "I've never used one of these."

Bob turned it on and told him, "Just work it and don't push too hard. You'll get the hang of it quick."

In no time Busta had everything smooth and looking like his trap, just bigger. A lot bigger. He took all the parts, jaws and springs, back to the table. Bob had made short work of the rest of the parts. With the help of a couple big clamps to compress the springs they put the trap together. They backed off the clamps and the jaws clenched together.

"Setting this thing might be tricky," Bob told him.

"Well let's see." Busta took the trap off the table. "Wow," he said. The trap was over three feet long and over five pounds. He laid it on the floor and put a heel on each spring like he was setting the one he had brought with him. That wouldn't work so he readjusted his feet now standing firmly on both springs. Busta didn't weigh enough to set the trap.

"I can't give you the clamps," said Bob. "But you might find one at the hardware store."

Busta put both feet, all his weight, on one spring. It went down far enough to set the trap. So, he sat there thinking for a minute. "I just need some rope. Hold on." Busta went outside to his pack to grab some rope. Back inside Bob had no idea what this flatlander, trapper wanna be was up to. When Busta stretched out the rope from hand to hand then doubled it and tied it in a knot, Bob chuckled. Busta slid the rope under the trap but just under the spring side. Its kind of made a big circle around the center of the trap. He picked up the rope on both sides of the jaws. Busta stepped back on the springs and squatted down as low as he could pulling the rope over his head, then trying to stand. By pushing down on the top of the springs with his feet and pulling up with the rope Busta was able to set the trap.

"Nice job," Bob said. "I didn't know what you were up to. Now that you got it set let's see if it works. I'll be right back. Don't let anyone step in it."

Bob was gone for a few minutes. He came back with Pete who was carrying a two-inch piece of wood about three feet long.

"So how did it come out?" Pete asked.

"Great," Busta said. "I thought I'd be a couple days. Can't believe it is finished already. Is that stick to see if it works?"

"Yup." Pete dropped the stick on the pan. Slam! The springs jumped up and the jaws came together breaking the two-inch piece of wood right in half. "I'd say she works. Maybe a little too well. Hopefully it doesn't do that to the bear. That wouldn't be good." Pete said.

"So, what do I owe you Pete? This thing should work great. If you are down a man I can stay around and help out. Work this off maybe?"

"Pete looked Busta up and down. "How did he do in the coal shed Bob?"

"Good. Everything is full."

Pete thinking Busta didn't have much money said, "You know it's been a long time since I had a good bear stew. How about you Bob?"

"Not for a couple years I think."

"So why don't you take that their trap and head back up in the woods. When you get that bear you bring back enough meat to feed the whole crew here a nice bear stew."

Busta was stunned and grateful at Pete's words. He never thought this would happen. "Thank you, Pete." Busta said as he shook his hand. "And thank you Bob. Nice work. I won't let you guys down. You'll have your bear stew."

Pete and Bob walked Busta out. As Busta crossed the little brook that went by the shop Bob looked at Pete and asked, "Do you think we will see him again?"

"Don't know. Don't care. I figured this was the easiest way to get rid of him. Don't know if I believe all of that story about the bear but I do think he is scared. He won't last long up here," Pete said walking away.

"So, what about the stew?" Bob asked.

Pete looked back at Bob, "You know I hate bear meat. It's too damn greasy and like chewing on your boot."

Bob laughing, "You're a good man Pete. You're a good man."

Busta headed for the road to the lake thinking it would be a long walk back to the dike. He would take a break at the edge of town. No sooner did he stop and take off his pack that a truck stopped. It was Paul, the same man that had given him a ride into town.

"Busta you headed back up to the lake? I didn't think you'd be going back so soon."

Busta was surprised to see that it was Paul that had stopped. "Yeah. I didn't expect to see you again today. You would not believe my day. That foundry is great. Can you believe I got the trap made in one day?"

"Really?"

"Yeah. Pete took me right in and set me up with Bob. We had it made in no time. Great bunch of guys." Busta told Paul all about his day at the foundry. It was a long trip to the lake for Paul. When they reached the lake, Paul wished Busta luck with the bear. Busta thanked him for the ride and headed for the canoe.

The sun had set but there was still enough light to see as he launched his canoe. He looked at his trap sticking out from his pack and felt a bit proud. He never thought he would see a trap made, let alone help to make one. This one was all his and he knew it would hold that bear. He wasn't sure where he was going to set it or what he was going to use for bait. He thought about just getting up and paddling for Sandy Stream then hike up over the ridge to the lean to. He saw the bear there before so it would be a good spot he figured; or maybe at the beaver dam or even Grant Brook. It has been there before too. He could just put another carcass on the rope and put the trap under it. That seemed like it would work. He figured the bear had set off all his traps and made the trip around his line. He needed to run and reset and re-bait the line but he needed to get the bear first. But how, and where?

When Busta reached his cabin, it was late and dark. Being tired from the long day, Busta stumbled getting out of his canoe and fell into the cold lake. Even though the water was only knee deep he was wet from head to toe. Stomping out of the water he grabbed the front of the canoe and drug it up onto the shore. Taking his pack in his hand he headed for the cabin. As he placed his foot on the first step, he knew something wasn't right. The door to the camp was open just a bit. Busta was certain it was closed when he left. He stopped and listened just to make sure he wasn't walking in to anything, especially that bear, seeing how his rifle was inside. He waited until he was sure it was safe then went inside. The camp had been ransacked. Nothing was where it was supposed to be. On his hands and knees, he finally found some matches, no longer in the box but spread all over the floor in front of the stove. Lighting one at a time, Busta let his eyes adjust to the dim light. He found that his oil lamp was still hanging on the center beam. He managed to get it down and lit, all the while looking around the camp making sure he was alone. As the lamp got brighter, he could see all the damage that had been done. Pots and pans no longer hung on the wall. His canned food was all over the floor, some with holes punched in them and leaking on to the floor. He was happy to see his rifle still hanging on the wall.

Busta walked over to the door, shut it and locked it. Turning around and looking at all the damage that had been done Busta was just downright mad. He went over and picked up some dry clothes off the floor and changed into them. Then he started to pick things up and put them back where they belonged. It was well after midnight when all the odds and ends were put back in place. Busta went to his cot flipping it over because of the tear, picked up his torn blanket, and laid down. It didn't take a very worn out Busta long to fall asleep.

The sunlight beaming through the window woke a sleepy Busta. It seemed as if he had just laid down. As he sat on his cot, he looked around the cabin. He saw claw marks on the floor and table and some by the sink. There were teeth marks on his chairs and the door. The bear had made a mess but didn't ruin anything. He just lost a little canned food. Busta was somewhat thankful. It could have been a lot worse he told himself. I can't believe that damn bear followed me to camp he thought to himself. What's next, he wondered. Busta got up and unlocked the door and opened it wide to let the morning sun warm his face. The bear was standing on his hind legs ten feet from the bottom step staring right at him. Busta slammed the door and ran for his rifle. When Busta looked back outside the bear was gone! It's still here somewhere nearby he thought so why not try to get him here.

Busta got dressed and made a plan. He would make a funnel with bait in the back and a stepping stick so the bear would get "funneled" into putting his foot right on the trap.

He went outside and looked around. He was looking for and found three trees in the shape of a triangle. These would work for the corner and hold the walls up. Busta got his axe and started to cut down some four-inch trees. He needed around twenty logs, some a little longer than the others. With the leftover spikes from building the cabin and a big hammer he started to build the walls. One on one side, then one on the other. When the walls were three feet high, he went to get his trap. He needed to see where to put it in the "v" so he could put his guide sticks in just the right place.

Busta cut some three-inch logs to a point and pounded them into the ground to narrow up the middle. Leaving a two-foot opening in the middle, he took another one and nailed it so that it was ten inches off the ground crossing the two-foot gap. This would make the bear step over it and right on to the pan of the trap. After that he put a couple more logs on the sides then added a roof; but only over the end where the trap and bait would be.

Now for the bait. What did he have left he wondered? Not much it seemed. The bear had taken all the scraps from behind the blowdown so Busta went for what the bear had destroyed inside the cabin. He grabbed all the cans that had been bitten in to and opened them up. He placed them way in the back of the "v" cubby. Busta didn't think that would be enough so he added some of that good 'ole stink bait. He had a good stash still left that the bear hadn't got in to. Finally, Busta set the trap. Slowly and carefully he worked it in to the cubby. He was extra careful not to set it off while going through the narrow opening. Laying it on in just the right place, he settled it into the soft dirt. He thought about covering it with sod and dirt but didn't want to take the chance of setting it off so he went back out and looked around. The woods were full of dry leaves. That would work he thought. He grabbed a couple big armfuls and covered the trap. The bait was in the back and the trap was set and covered. Now he just needed to make sure the bear couldn't get away with the trap. Six feet of chain and some nuts and bolts would make sure of that. Busta wrapped one end around the tree and the other around the trap. This would hold the bear right there. He wouldn't be going anywhere. A couple more armfuls of leaves to cover the chains and the set was finished.

All this took a lot longer than Busta had anticipated. After he was done, he got a bite to eat and looked around. "Well if I'm going to run that line again, I'm going to need some bait. Damn bear ate all my meat up so I guess I gotta get some fish." Busta grabbed his pole and hopped in the canoe. It wasn't long and he had fish for bait and some for supper too. He paddled back to camp long before dark. He didn't want to be surprised by that bear. Landing the canoe, he kept a close eye on the woods. Not seeing anything or hearing anything but the wind and the loons, Busta took five more casts out. He caught some sunfish and some chub. These he would use for fresh bait at the bear set. All the guts from the fish he had planned to eat for supper went in to the cubby also.

Busta thought he would have the bear in the morning but wanted to be ready to run the trap line just in case. He loaded his pack with bait and his wool blanket and a few other items that he might need to remake some of the sets that were destroyed. The canoe was ready by the lake and supper was on the stove. Busta began to relax. He ate his dinner and took care of the dishes. Still no bear. The rifle was loaded and placed beside the bed. Busta wasn't going to get caught off guard again. His mind was on the trap line as he settled down and climbed into bed.

Busta awoke in the morning peacefully with no sign of the bear around the camp or trap. He set off in the canoe for Grant Brook and the beginning of his line. Cool temperatures had made some ice along the shore but the lake was open and calm. It made for easy paddling. He stopped on the point and remade the two sets. He baited both with the fish he had caught the day before. Then he went back in the canoe and on up to the beaver dam, reaching it with no time to spare. He landed the canoe and pulled it up into the woods. Looking around he saw a couple bear tracks but they looked to be old. Busta went out on to the dam and remade that set and all the others. Donning his pack, he set out across the ridge remaking each and every set the bear had destroyed. Busta was making good time. The trail was getting better and more passable with each trip. Even with stopping and remaking or refreshing each set it didn't seem to slow him down any. He reached the lean-to and had a fire going before dark. He had time to spare so he decided to add to the wood pile. A few trips to the blown down tree and the wood pile was back to normal. He made a couple more trips just in case he might have a visitor. He didn't want to run low again. With extra logs on, Busta settled down by the fire. He didn't want to be caught off guard so the rifle was loaded and more logs placed on to the fire. Laying down he thought about the trip back to the canoe and what he might find back at camp and where the bear might be but it didn't keep him from falling asleep.

Sometime in the middle of the night a bawling cry echoed across the lake. It woke Busta and sent a shiver down his spine. He had never heard such a sound. There it was again far off in the distance carried by the wind but still there. A bawling cry but not like a baby. This was something different. Haunting. Long and slow.

Busta stood with the gun in hand looking in to the blackness of the night. He could still hear the cries as he added more wood to the fire. It went on and on with every gust of the wind and every snap of the fire. Busta jumped. He tried to stay calm and not let his imagination get the best of him but he wouldn't be sleeping anymore tonight. Busta kept feeding the fire and walking around in circles waiting for the sun to rise. As the night went on Busta thought he could hear people hollering way off in the distance. He wondered what was going on and if anyone was hurt but it could just be the wind he thought, or his imagination.

The horizon started to lighten and the sky was turning a crimson red. Busta thought about the old saying, red sky in the morning, sailors take warning. He wondered what the day would bring. When the sun broke the horizon Busta headed back into the woods. Up and over the ridge remaking each set just as he had done the day before. All the way back to the canoe he kept an eye in the woods and over his shoulder. The sounds from the night were still in his head and made him a little uneasy.

Busta reached the beaver dam in the middle part of the afternoon. No animals were in the traps so he headed for his canoe. He stopped in his tracks when he saw the canoe. It wasn't where he had left it up in the woods but instead it was out in the open and covered in what looked like blood. Busta walked up to the canoe and saw two big holes smashed in the bottom. Claw and bite marks were everywhere. Bear tracks were all over the ground but something wasn't right. His paddle was bit in half. There was no way the canoe would float. It would need at least a full day's repair if not two. Busta stood and looked at the canoe. A raven cawed and Busta jumped, breaking his stare.

Wading the stream, Busta tripped and fell. Now wet and a half hour from camp he started the long walk back. It seemed as though every stump and every other branch tripped him or snagged his clothing. His pack grew heavier with each minute that passed.

Rounding the edge of the clearing at camp what Busta saw left him speechless. The first thing he noticed was claw marks and blood on the front door of the camp. He glanced over at the set he had made for the bear. It was all but gone. Sticks and logs were strung all over but there was no sign of the bear. At least not at first glance.

Busta headed straight for the front door. He needed to get his pack and wet clothes off. Inside the cabin with the door locked and his rifle within arm's reach, he changed his clothes and got the fire going. The sun had started to set and Busta fell asleep right at the kitchen table.

He awoke in the morning with his hand still on his rifle. Slowly he opened the door, looking and listening for any sign of the bear. Nothing. Busta could relax a bit so he decided to cook some breakfast. After eating and taking care of the dishes he stepped outside to have a look at the claw marks and blood on the door and porch. With round circles of blood Busta didn't understand what he was looking at until he got to what was left of the set. Even though it was completely destroyed the trap was still there and still attached to the chain. Even though the trees bark was shredded and all clawed up it was big enough to keep the trap in place.

Busta reached down and pulled the trap free from the debris. He dropped it to the ground when he saw the bears front left foot still held in place. He remembered Pete's words: "That wouldn't be good." And Busta was sure this wasn't going to be.

He pulled the foot out of the trap comparing it in size to his own. It was just about the same size. He decided to reset the trap and remake the set but he wouldn't get so elaborate this time. Most of the bait was still in the corner at the base of the tree so Busta gathered the logs up and made a "V", leaving one log on the ground so the bear would step over it. He piled one end of the logs behind the bait and kind of fanned the other ends on the ground. About that time Busta heard someone behind him.

Chapter Four
The Hoof-ma-goof

"Hey, everything ok over here?"

Busta turned around and saw Ray, who was a Native American Indian and a native to Maine, who lived across the cove.

"We heard some awful sounds coming from over here last night," Ray said as he landed his boat on shore. "Me and the Mrs. came outside camp and hollered out but no one answered back, just an awful bawling sound. What was going on?"

Busta had never talked to Ray but had seen him around the lake.

"Well," Busta began, "I am fine. Sorry for the commotion. I was out on my line and I caught a bear here at camp."

"Caught a bear?" Ray asked. "In what?"

Busta looking at Ray and feeling a little ashamed said, "I had a bear destroying my sets and he followed me back here to camp. Started busting up things here so I went to town and got a bear trap. I guess I should have stayed home one more night."

"Bear trap from town?" Ray asked. "Where in town did you find one?"

"The Foundry," Busta said. "We made it last week. I only had it set two nights. I stayed home the first night. Should have stayed home another. Now I am out my canoe and I still haven't got rid of this damn bear."

"But you said you caught it. That must have been the bawling we heard. Awful noise."

"Ya I caught it a little too well. The trap was a little too big you might say. It took his foot off," Busta said, disgusted.

"Hoof ma goof," Ray mumbled. "You must right this. You can't have one of these running around."

"One of what? A three-legged bear?" Busta scoffed. "It will never survive."

"Hoof ma goof," Ray repeated. "You created it. You need to get rid of it before anything else happens. This is bad. A wounded bear changes its temper. It gets mad, angry...and smarter than one might think."

Busta could see Ray was serious but replied, "It's just a bear. He will come back and he will step in that trap, (pointing toward the set) and I catch him again except this time I will be here and I will shoot the damn thing."

"Oh, he'll be back and I hope you do get him but I doubt it. I think you are just going to make him mad. Real mad," Ray said as he got back in his boat. "If you do need help just holler. Real loud. And I would get rid of that foot too. He will be looking for it."

"Ya, I'm sure he will," Busta said. "I'll be waiting!"

Ray started for home in his boat and Busta turned back to his camp. He stood looking around, taking in all the damage and mess. Looking over to the set and seeing the severed foot laying on the ground, he knew Ray had seen it. He walked over and picked it up. Holding it he felt a little ashamed. Busta drew a heavy breath and sighed. He walked down to the blown down tree with spade in hand and buried the foot.

Walking back to camp he was thinking what to do next. He knew by now the bear was going to run his line all the way to the lean to and back. All the sets would be trashed and would have to be set again. He figured the bear would be back tonight and if not, he would wait one more day before going out and running the line himself.

Busta had some time to kill, so to speak. He would spend it stacking some winter wood, fishing for a little suppa, and cleaning up around camp, all the while keeping his gun close at hand. The rest of the day passed with no sign of the bear.

He woke the next day and still no bear. The trap was empty and Busta couldn't help but wonder if the bear was still alive. He decided not to wait another night. Filling his pack and dressing for the weather, he would head for his busted-up canoe. It was going to be a long walk all the way to the lean to.

Reaching the canoe, Busta took a good look around surveying everything. The tracks. The busted-up canoe. He was thinking on the way back to camp he might drag it back. Turning into the woods Busta could still see blood on the leaves, but only here and there. Walking with the gun ready, he headed for his trap line expecting the worst.

Reaching his first set he found another "coon" waiting. Busta was surprised. He didn't think he would get anything in his traps. He figured the bear would follow the same routine, eat and destroy the set. He was happy to see the coon. He took care of it and loaded it into his pack and started down the trail.

He reached the second set and still no sign of the bear. The trap was still set and bait undisturbed. On down the trail he went, stopping at each set. He found a martin in one and a fisher in another. Just before the turn down the ridge to the lean-to a coyote was sitting there waiting for him to come along. Now this is better Busta thought as he loaded the coyote on the top of his pack.

It was late in the afternoon when he reached the lean-to. Busta didn't waste any time. The sun would be setting soon. He got a good fire going and then started to skin the pine marten. Next, the coon. He would use some for bait and a little for a snack later, slow roasting the hind legs on the campfire. The last thing he would take care of was the coyote. It would take the longest. He would finish it by campfire light.

After everything that happened, Busta still wouldn't be sleeping well tonight. He would be thinking about the bear and where it could be and if it was still alive.

Busta wrapped up bits of the coon that he could use for bait then he took what was left along with the coyote and martin over to an uprooted tree and buried them. He didn't want the smell of fresh meat or blood in the air tonight. A few more logs on the fire and Busta was ready for a long night. With his back against the wall of the lean to and rifle in hand, Busta waited for morning.

It got cold that night. The torn wool blanket along with his own still didn't keep him very warm. As dawn cracked, he could see the glimmer of frost on everything. He let the fire die down and made sure everything was packed for the long walk back to camp. Rolling the furs up, fur side inside out, he laid them on the bottom of his pack then carefully rolled the fisher in the pack. Bait and blanket next then up the trail he went.

On the way back to the canoe Busta picked up another martin. He had to remake two sets, but not because of the bear this time. A coon he thought on one set and a coyote must have pulled out of the other. He was glad to see no sign of the bear, his hoof-ma-goof.

He made it to the beaver dam and his busted-up canoe with still no sign of the bear. His canoe was in rough shape. One big hole right in the bottom and a couple claw marks here and there. Busta knew a few tricks however. He started a little fire then went to look for what he needed to fix it. A good piece of white birch bark and a big gob of spruce gum. Heating the spruce gum on the fire would make it workable. Put a stick in the hole and drip the spruce gum around it and presto, water tight. He would use the birch bark like a bandaid. Once that was done, he rolled it over and put it in the water. It leaked a little but would get him home.

Landing the canoe back at camp, Busta felt relieved. A full two days and no sign of the hoof-ma-goof. Well almost. The camp had been hit again. Busta looked toward the set where the bear trap was. The set was destroyed. Logs were thrown everywhere and all the bait was gone. The trap lay right on top of the ground twisted and broken. The jaws were twisted and one spring broken right where it met the jaws. The pan of the trap was torn clear off. Busta just stood looking, staring, in disbelief. How could a bear do this to that trap? He turned to the camp and saw that the front door was wide open. Busta walked up on to the porch and looked inside. It was just like before but much worse. More things broken, more things torn, and more things destroyed.

The sun was setting. Busta locked the door and put the wood stove back together. Despite everything he still had a fisher and pine martin to take care of, not to mention furs to flesh and get on a stretcher. It was going to be a long night. He took care of the two that he had to skin, then fleshed them all one at a time and got them on to the stretchers.

It snowed that night. When Busta woke, three inches of wet, sticky snow covered the ground. He thought, now is my chance to get him. Busta put on his woollies and coat and grabbed his rifle. Out the door he went thinking his three-legged bear would be easy to track and catch up to. All he had to do was find a track.

Busta headed for the beaver dam on foot. He would run his whole line but not stop to check or tend to any sets. Only thing he was looking for was a sign of the hoof-ma-goof.

He made it to the dam in no time. With no sign there he went a quarter mile back around the pond with still no sign. Crossing the damn, he headed up on the ridge. Nothing. He took the back way to the lean to sure he would see something but no sign anywhere. He took a break at the lean to. It was just afternoon. With no supplies he wouldn't be able to stay there.

Busta knew he had to get back to camp before dark so he didn't rest long. He would head straight for camp by heading down to the lake and walking the shore line. Tomorrow he would try another route. Making it back to camp just before dark, wet and tired, Busta couldn't help but think of where he had been and where that bear could be.

He got a fire going in the old stove. The cabin was warm in no time. He checked and tended to the furs on the stretchers making sure everything was drying good, then changed into a dry union suit. Loading the wood stove one more time before he crawled into bed, where is that dam bear? is all he could think about.

The next morning the snow was still on the ground and it was a bit colder than the day before. Busta set out in a different direction. He went straight behind the cabin this time. With rifle in hand and a bit of jerky in his pocket, it was going to be another long day trying to track a bear in the snow with no tracks in sight.

At the top of the ridge behind camp Busta stopped and thought some more. Could that bear know whether he was at camp or not? That didn't matter. He just needed to "cut a track". He would make a bigger loop today. Down the ridge and well above the beaver pond on Grant Brook is where he crossed, still with no sign.

It was still quite early in the day. As he crossed the brook, he could see the ridge and where his trap line was and the route, he had taken the day before. He was on the west side of the big main ridge between Grant Brook and Sandy Stream. "Well," Busta said to himself, "I'm going to head around to the back side and see if this damn hoof-ma-goof is hiding over there."

So around the backside he went. Busta had never ventured over to this side. It was thick with fur and spruce and cedar growing up so tight together you couldn't walk through. As he was circling one of the cedar, he noticed a tunnel through the growth that looked to be four feet tall and almost three feet wide. "Well let's see where this goes," Busta said quietly. He had to duck and squat a little but it was easy walking. The tunnel led to a trail carved right in to the ground from years of use. He saw tracks of all kinds of animals. Deer, moose, but no three-legged bear. The trail led to another tunnel and it led to a hemlock grove. This one looked familiar and Busta knew right where he was. He was in the saddle. The trap line was just to the other side. Just a short walk and he was looking right at one of his sets. The fur was gone and the set was busted up and covered with snow. This had happened a couple of days ago he thought. It must have happened the day before the storm. Somehow, he and the bear had just missed each other that day. "That's it!" Busta said. "Damn that bear! Damn that hoof-ma-goof. I've had enough!"

Busta headed back to camp. He had an uneasy night. What to do? He knew he had to go get the rest of his line. How many more animals did he lose while he was out looking for the bear, he wondered.

At first light Busta headed out. He wanted to pull the whole line. It was going to be a long trip. He had to break ice to get to the canoe out in the lake. That was just the beginning of the day, and it wouldn't get any easier. No animals were in the traps on the point so that didn't slow him down too much. At the beaver dam he had two muskrats, much to his surprise. He pulled all the traps and laid them in the canoe then up over the ridge he went. Just what he thought; bait gone and traps set off. He must have just missed the bear when he came by that night because they were all set when he left.

With each sprung trap and destroyed fur Busta got madder and madder. By the time he reached the cut off to the lean-to he was very upset, to say the least. Not a fur in the pack. He was at a pace that a young man would have a hard time keeping up with. Breaking a sweat and at a steady long step pace he just walked on by making the whole loop back to the canoe just before dark. He dropped his heavy pack to the ground, full of traps but no fur, then loaded everything in to the canoe for the paddle back to camp. The ride back felt twice as long as normal.

Busta reached camp well after dark. He pulled the canoe up on to the shore thankful that the ice he broke this morning hadn't froze back up. With rifle in hand he looked around to see if the hoof-ma-goof had returned. It was difficult to see in the dark of the night. The clouds were blocking out the light from the quarter moon. He walked slow and listened intensely but when he reached the front door of the cabin, he could see that it was still closed.

Busta went in and got the oil lantern lit and went back outside. He hung the lantern on the nail at the top of the stairs then headed back to the canoe to get his pack and traps. He still felt uneasy.

Reaching the canoe with rifle in hand, Busta took hold of it by the bow with one hand and drug it all the way to the cabin. "There. I'm done," Busta said, but nothing was farther from the truth. "I'm not setting another trap until I know that damn Hoof-ma-goof is dead!" He took the lantern down and went in to the cabin. Looking up in the rafters at the furs he could see the bear had not destroyed it. He thought he would have had a good year. Right now, though he was plum tired. Busta got the fire going in the wood stove and then laid down. He was almost asleep as his head hit the pillow.

It was snowing a wet snow, almost rain, and the wind was blowing and swirling around when Busta woke to the sound of a tree dropping on the roof. The rifle almost went off when he grabbed it off the floor. Blinking and rubbing his eyes, Busta looked around. He got out of bed and added a log or two to the coals in the wood stove then looked outside. "Wind? Yup. Rain? Yup. Snow? Yup. Welcome to Maine! I'm going back to bed!" Busta said as he did just that. He fell back asleep and woke just before noon. "Well it's about time to get something in my gut," Busta said as he got out of bed once again. He added more wood to the stove and looked around. Not much was left. The bear had destroyed almost everything in the cabin as far as the food was concerned. Busta hadn't realized how low his food supply had gotten but he did have fur and it was time to get rid of it. The fur monger or broker, (the man that went to town buying up ready fur) should be in town soon. Busta began taking his furs down and getting them ready for market. He wiped off the little bit of grease and trimmed up the legs and bottom so they didn't look ragged. He bundled up the pine marten with the fisher and mink and rolled them up in the largest beaver pelt he had. This would keep them safe on the the trip into town. Each beaver pelt got rolled up and tied off along with the raccoons. The coyote and fox he would let hang on the outside of his pack so he could show them off.

Once the fur was all put up and ready to go Busta looked back outside. Yup, still windy with that rain-snow mix. Well I'm not heading in to town in this mess he thought so he put on his coat and went out to the canoe to gather up his traps and bring them in to the cabin. He set them down on the floor by the stove. The slush and ice quickly began to melt away. One by one Busta inspected each trap making sure the bear hadn't bent or broken any one of them. Some of them still had the foot of what he had caught in them and what the hoof-ma-goof bear had eaten.A martin here. A coon there. All Busta could see was fur that he didn't get to cash in and that meant money he didn't make.

He put them in groups of six and tied them together with a little piece of wire. This way Busta could use his long "V" topped pole and hang them up in the rafters on the nails where the fur had just hung. By the time he was done it was late in the afternoon and the rain-snow mix had turned to just snow. Busta went out and brought in some more wood and flipped over the canoe. Something he should have done when he pulled the traps out because now it was wet and heavy with ice and slush. If he had done it earlier it probably would have melted but as the sun dropped it would freeze.

Busta brought in the wet wood and piled it up by the stove. It wouldn't take but a day and it would be ready to go.

Camp was clean again and everything put away as it started to get dark so Busta laid out everything for the trip in to town the next day then he went to bed.

Chapter Five
Town

Busta got up early the next morning knowing he had a long day ahead of him. He dressed for the long walk in to town. He wasn't expecting a ride. He stepped outside. Three to four inches of frozen snow covered the ground. Looking at the canoe he shook his head. "I knew I should have rolled that thing over when I saw the first flake," Busta said to himself. He walked down to it. The icy snow was clinging to it everywhere inside and out. Busta drug it over to the wood pile and rolled one end up on to it. He thought the sun might dry it out while he was in town. After that while he was right there, he grabbed an armload of wood and went back in to the cabin. He looked around one more time seeing if he needed anything. He grabbed his list of items to replenish the camp then put on his pack. With rifle in hand he went out the door. Fifteen minutes later he was on the road to town. He had forgot about his hoof-ma-goof and was feeling a little proud. He had done what he had set out to do: survive the Maine woods and trap the land. He knew he could have had a better year but for his first-year trapping in Maine he was happy.

It was still early in the morning and Busta was hoping that someone might happen by to give him a ride. It wasn't long and he could hear a truck coming down the road. Busta turned to look then took a heavy sigh and looked back in the direction he was walking, not because he didn't want a ride, but because of who it was coming down the road and what it was going to lead to. It was Ray, his neighbor from across the cove. The man that named his bear the hoof-ma-goof. It was a long walk and Busta wasn't going to refuse a ride from anyone, not even Ray.

"Can I give you a lift to town?" Ray asked. "I see you with those furs. You picked a good day to head in to town. The fur monger is in town and buying up everything that people bring him."

"That's just what I wanted to hear," Busta said.

"Toss your fur and pack on back next to mine. That's where I was headed myself," Ray told him.

Busta rolled off his pack and slung it over in to the bed of the truck and stood back amazed at what he saw. Ray had nearly three times the fur he did.

"Well don't just stand there gawking. Get in," Ray told him. "We have places to get to."
Busta got in and just looked at Ray then turned and watched the road not saying a word.

"Well," Ray said, breaking the silence. "You got something to say just say it."

"How did you get so much fur?" Busta blurted out.

Ray laughed and said, "I've been here awhile and know where to go and how long to stay before moving to a new spot. I see you got some skins."

"Ya," Busta answered. "But nothing like what you have."

"I run three different lines," Ray explained. "One by boat, one by this old truck and a canoe, and one over the ridge. that I check on every fourth day. My wife takes care of the fur while I am out on the line and has supper ready when I get back. It's good this way. I talked to Johnny. He asked if you could use my old lean to over by Sandy Stream. Told him I didn't mind. I hadn't trapped over there in a year and thought it might do you some good."

"That's your lean to I've been using?" Busta said in disbelief.

"Yea. Built it about eight years back. How is it holding up?"

"Not too bad. Could use a little work now though but it works fine. Must be your blanket hanging on the back wall."

"Yeah."

"Thanks for leaving it behind. It came in handy one of those cold nights."

"Well that's why I left it behind," Ray told him. It was quiet in the truck for a while as he let that sink in.

"So, when did you talk to Johnny?" Busta asked. "He never told me that lean to was yours."

"Oh, I think it was the first day you started on your cabin. Don't know why but Johnny thought...I don't know what Johnny thought," Ray said.

"What do you mean?" Busta asked.

"Well I think he he could see something in you. And, well, he thought he could help you out. Johnny knows the land and the people. He just can't get around good," Ray said. "He knew I wasn't going to be using that lean to. That's why he told you where it was."

Busta just sat there taking it all in. He never knew that Ray had helped him out and he was feeling belittled.

"Well I guess I need to thank you Ray. I didn't think you like me, being from away and all. I guess I had you wrong."

"Listen and listen good Busta. If I don't like you or if you did something I don't care for, there would be no guessing. You would know," Ray told him as he laughed and winked. Ray then turned and looked at Busta straight in the face and in an unmistakable tone said, "I mean it."

Busta had a new respect for Ray but he knew it wouldn't last long. There it was, just as soon as Busta started to relax. "So," Ray said. "That bear. You got him, right? He's dead right?"

"No," Busta replied. "He kept raiding my traps but I never got to see him. I tried to track him down after the snow but I never found a track. I don't know where he is."

"He isn't far," Ray said and never spoke another word all the way in to town.

Busta could see it agitated Ray and he tried to explain how hard he looked and that he let his line go for days while he was hunting for that bear but Ray just sat there silent, staring down the road. Busta turned away and gave up trying to explain. It was a very quiet ride after that.

Once they reached town Ray pulled over. He sat there looking straight ahead. Busta got the message. He opened the door and got out. He grabbed his pack load of furs off the back of the truck then leaned back inside to get his rifle.

"You didn't say where that fur monger was going to be today did ya Ray?" Busta asked, not expecting a reply.

Ray turned and said, "Nope I didn't, but I think even you might be able to track him down. Ask around. I got things to do."

And with that Busta said, "Thanks for the ride Ray and I am sorry I didn't get that bear." As he closed the door, he heard Ray say, "Not as sorry as you're going to be."

Busta wanted to ask what he meant by that but Ray drove off. Feeling a little sick to his stomach, Busta wondered what else this day would bring. He figured someone down at the town office would know all about the fur auction or where he might find the fur monger. As Busta went under the railroad tracks he could hear someone hollering up a storm. Someone is getting an earful he thought and as he walked down the road, he could see just who it was. It was Bob and Pete. Ray had them both outside the foundry and was just carrying on. Busta couldn't make out what was being said but he knew it wasn't good and he figured it was about him. Then, as if on cue, Ray stopped talking and all three turned and looked at Busta. Ray stomped away, Bob went back in to the building and Pete just watched Busta walk on by. Right then Busta knew the day wasn't going to get any better.

When he reached the town office, he saw Ray's truck parked outside. There was a sign out front that read: 'Buying Furs Today'. Busta looked but didn't see any furs on the back of Ray's truck. Must be the right place he thought. Busta went inside.

"You can leave that rifle here sir," The elderly clerk said in a polite but stern way.

"Oh. Almost forgot I was carrying it. Sorry, here you go," Busta said, almost embarrassed. As he looked around the clerk said, "Upstairs to your right then left at the top."

"Oh, thanks."

As he walked around the corner and up the stairs, he could hear men talking. One voice stood out. It was Ray. When he reached the top of the stairs, he could see Ray talking to three men. As soon as Ray saw Busta he stopped talking. All three men turned to look.

"That's him," Ray said, and the four men parted ways. They all walked back to their piles of fur and began priming them for sale. Busta walked down the hall and got the cold shoulder from everyone there. One big man in a green plaid wool coat stopped him before he got too far down. "There is a line," He said. "And you're at the end, so back up."

"Ok," Busta said. "This is my first time here. I didn't know. My name is..."

"Busta!" The man snapped back.

"Ya."

"Heard all about you and I didn't like what I heard either."

Busta turned and went back to the beginning of the hall. Waiting and watching. This one talking to that one and that one talking to those ones. Busta couldn't help but think they were all talking about him. As more local trappers arrived, they walked right by him. Shaking hands, smiling,saying hello and such. Busta knew he was outnumbered and out of place. He kept still and stayed in place. One by one they all left. Even Ray wouldn't acknowledge him as he walked by. Busta got the point. He knew Ray was upset about that damned bear.

Busta made his way down the hall and finally into the main room. Fur was piled up high everywhere. Busta was last in line and when the man in front of him walked away the fur monger looked at him and turned his back. Busta waited a minute because he could see that he was taking care of the last man's furs but then he began to pack up. That was enough.

"So, what is going on here?" Busta asked. "I have furs I need to sell and you bought everyone else's."

The man stopped and turned to look at Busta. He looked him up and down but didn't say a word.

The man had a look on him that Busta couldn't figure out.

"So?" Busta said as he wondered how to proceed. This man is here now buying fur and he didn't want to miss the opportunity. He had to befriend this man and get to the bottom of what is going on. "Will you look at my furs and maybe tell me what is going on?" Busta asked ever so politely.

"Well," the man said. "I don't know these men and some are upset with you. They said they would boycott me next year if I bought your furs. I can't have that you understand. There is going to be someone outside watching to see if you come out with or without furs."

"But why? What did I do to all those men?" Busta asked.

"Well, the said you would ask that," The fur monger looked at Busta and said, "Do you know what a hoof-ma-goof is? They all say you created one and they would be lucky to have any fur in their traps next year. I'm not sure what it is and don't know that I want to. But I do know..."

He stopped and looked at Busta making sure that he was paying close attention.

"These men blame you for it and they are mad."

"I trapped a bear and it lost a foot. Ray called it a hoof-ma-goof. I don't know why."

The fur monger cut Busta off. "The bear lives?" he asked.

"I guess so. I mean, yeah. I tried to track it down but I never saw it. Ray said it was up to me to kill it but if I can't find it how am I supposed to do that?"

"Well that explains a lot," The fur monger replied. "You see, that bear is going to raid every cabin, every trap, every easy meal it can find. That's why they are all mad. Nobody told you that?"

"Nope. Ray just said I made it and I need to kill it. Didn't say why."

"You see, this bear is going to learn, and learn fast, and it isn't going to be good."

"I've heard that before," Busta said.

"Well this is where it starts," The fur monger told him.

"So, you aren't going to buy my fur because of some damn bear?" Busta said, trying not to get any madder than he already was.

"Well I told you someone will be watching when you leave. But they won't be watching you all night. I will look them over tonight but you ARE going to leave with them. If you like the price I offer you meet me at midnight and we will swap for cash. Deal?"

"Well I don't have much of a choice, do I?" Busta said.

The fur monger looked over Busta's furs and made a good offer so they agreed to meet just on the edge of town so no one would see the exchange. The man looked at Busta and said just before they parted, "The way I see it, you have two choices. You can take the money and run or you can hunt that hoof-ma-goof down in the spring. Either way, I wouldn't want to be in your boots.

Busta packed up his furs and walked downstairs. The clerk's office was closed. His rifle was still behind bars. 'Open at eight o'clock' the sign read. Busta was getting more and more irritated. Now what? he thought. Busta had some time to kill and he hadn't eaten all day so he decided to go down the street and get something to eat but then he remembered he didn't have any money. He walked back upstairs where the fur monger was still packing up.

"Hey, if I help you pack up your truck could I get an advance so I can get something to eat while I wait around tonight?" Busta asked.

"Well I guess I could do that seeing how no one else is here to help. Did you see anyone watching from outside?"

"I never even made it outside. I realized I didn't have any money or anything to barter with so I came back up here."

"Here. How is a couple of dollars now?" the man asked.

Busta took the money and started down the stairs, bundles of furs over his shoulders. Outside, he placed them in the man's truck carefully so as not to damage them in any way. As he left the truck to go get more fur, Busta, noticed Ray and a group of men outside the tavern just up the street. Busta made three more trips up and down the stairs before all the furs were loaded. Except his.

Chapter Six
The Tavern

"Thanks for the help," the man said to Busta. "You understand that we will meet later?"

"I hope so," Busta replied.

Busta grabbed his fur and pack and headed back downstairs and outside. He looked up to the street at the tavern. Ray's truck was still there. It was getting late and Busta needed to hear what Ray had to say so he headed for the tavern. Just as Busta got there two men came out. With one staring him down, the other said, "I wouldn't do that if I were you."

"Do what?" Busta asked.

"Go inside," the man replied as he walked away.

Busta didn't have anywhere else to wait. He walked in. Just to his left there was an empty table in the corner. He walked over and took his pack off, turned the chair so his back was to the wall and settled in. The bartender walked over. "We don't want any trouble here," he told him.

"Not looking for any. Just some food, whiskey, and a bed for the night."

"Food and drink I can do. We will have to see about a room later."

The bartender went back to the bar and grabbed a glass and a bottle then made his way back over. "You need to pay for the food and drink before you eat."

Busta just looked at him. The bartender stood there holding the glass and bottle.

"So, you need to see my money?" Busta said.

"Yup," the bartender replied.

Busta lay out the two dollars the fur monger had just given him. The man looked down at the table and took the money slyly, palming the cash in his hand then sliding it in his pocket. "And a room he said," but only loud enough for Busta to hear.

Busta poured himself a shot and sat there sipping it. It wasn't off the top shelf. This stuff was strong and burned all the way down. Busta wasn't a big drinker but tonight he thought he would play the part.

Ray stayed on the other side of the room, a group of men always around him, laughing, toasting and looking at Busta. Not all at once but enough so he got the point. They weren't looking to make friends.

A woman came out from the kitchen and brought Busta a meal. As she set it on the table, without looking up, she told him, "Eat and go to your room. Room 3, out back and up the stairs."

Busta just looked at her. She turned back to the bar and walked away. As he looked down at the plate of food she had just left, there beside the fork and knife was a key with a number three on the tag. Busta slid the key in his pocket, looking to make sure no one was watching.

Busta was just finishing his meal when who should walk in but Johnny Blueberry. Johnny walked straight to the bar. No need to look around. He ordered a drink, said hi to a couple of guys, gave Ray a friendly "hey" and settled in a seat at the bar. The bartender kept a close watch on Busta. He noticed Busta watching Johnny. As he poured Johnny his drink, he nodded toward Busta. "You know him?" He asked.

Johnny turned to see Busta sitting in the corner, furs beside him in his pack, not looking so good. "Yeah I know him. That's Busta. He's a friend of mine."

"Watch who you call a friend Johnny." A voice came out of the group of men behind him. Johnny turned to look. Almost every man in the tavern was looking at him. He turned and looked at Busta. Johnny got up off his stool and made his way to Busta's table.

"Mind if I join you?" Johnny asked as he pulled up a chair.

"Not so sure you want to do that," Busta told him as he looked over Johnny's shoulder. "You're not going to make any friends sitting over here with me."

"Oh, I know all those men. They just don't know you."

"Oh, I think they do. I think Ray has got them all filled in as to who I am," Busta said as he glared at Ray.

"What do you mean?" Johnny looked over his shoulder only to see half a dozen men looking back at him. He turned back and said, "What's going on?" Busta looked at Johnny and said, "Well that's something you need to ask Ray."

"No, I am asking you."

"Well," Busta replied, "Ray is pissed at me. I trapped a bear and didn't get to kill it. It got away with three legs."

"A hoof-ma-goof," Johnny interrupted.

"Ya. That's what he called it. Now he is pissed and telling everybody, I guess. Just look at them all," Busta said, pointing to the group of men around Ray.

"You got a place to stay tonight?" Johnny asked. "You're not heading back to camp, are you?"

"No, I've made arrangements."

"Ok. When I get up, I am going to talk to Ray. When I do, you get out of here. We will talk later about this. I will find you tomorrow, ok?"

Busta nodded. He took another bite out of his meal then poured him and Johnny a drink. "To the Maine woods and the damn hoof-ma-goof," Busta toasted. Johnny couldn't believe he just had the nerve to do that. "I'm saving your ass. Now tell me off and get."

Johnny grabbed his drink, jumped up, and barked back so everyone in the tavern could hear. "You dumb son of a bitch! You have put everyone at risk. Everyone!"

Johnny turned and walked straight through the group of men and all eyes followed him. No one but the bartender saw Busta grab his pack and walk right out the front door. He hurried down the little alley and went upstairs to room 3.

"Ray looked at Johnny. "You're friend ain't that smart."

Johnny turned to look at Busta, but Busta was gone. "Smarter than you think," Johnny said back to Ray, stepping aside so he could see that Busta had left.

"Funny," Ray said. "Good trick but you know what a hoof-ma-goof can do. He has got to go." Johnny asked, "Who? Busta or the bear?"

"Both!" Ray barked back. "Both. Busta has to get that bear before he gets someone and if he doesn't, he will be next. You get my drift Johnny?"

"Johnny looked at Ray and finished his drink. As he turned away Ray said, "You let your friend know what I said won't ya Johnny?"

"Johnny walked right through the crowd and out the front door. He tried to think where Busta might be but he wasn't going to look around. He knew someone would be watching him; so back down tin can alley he went, back to his room.

Busta laid down on the bed. He could hear Ray through the floor but couldn't make out what he was saying. He knew it was about him though and it wasn't good. He kept an eye on the clock. Midnight couldn't come fast enough.

Slowly the noise from downstairs died down. Busta thought about taking a nap but was afraid he would sleep right through until morning. That wouldn't be good at all. He started pacing back and forth. What am I going to do he wondered? Don't want to spend all winter up there in that cabin with everyone outside of it mad at me and I can't stay in town. Busta saw some paper and pen on the desk. Right then it hit him. He sat down and wrote Johnny a letter.

To my friend Johnny,

It is with deepest regret that I write you this letter. I must leave tonight for home. I have received a letter from my sister. My father has been stricken ill and mother can't take care of the business at hand. I would have told you earlier but had not yet read the letter. I am leaving the camp to you seeing how you helped to build it and were so helpful to me while I was here. I'm sure you will see the bear this spring if he survives the winter, which I doubt. Please take care and don't let the hoof-ma-goof get ya.

Sincerely,
Busta.

P.S. The last part was a joke and my rifle is at the town hall. It too is yours.

Busta folded up the letter and dripped some candle wax on the edge to seal it. 'Please give this to my friend Johnny Blueberry' he wrote on the front. He laid it out so anyone who walked in the room would see it. He put his pack on and left the room. He went down the stairs and back out the alley. He looked around and saw no one so he hurried across the road and made his way to the edge of town where he hoped to meet the fur monger once more.

Midnight headlights made their way up the hill. The truck pulled over and Busta stepped out from the shadow. "Wasn't sure you were going to make it," Busta said.

"I could say the same thing," The man replied. "Just throw your furs in back. I have your money right here."

Busta threw furs, pack and all, in to the truck then climbed in the cab. "Let's go."

"Go where?" the fur monger asked.

"Wherever you need to be tomorrow morning," Busta said, motioning for him to start driving.

"That wasn't part of the deal. I'm not taking on anyone."

"Just get me to the next town and point me south," Busta snapped. "I can't stay here and I don't have any way out so if you don't mind, let's be on our way."

The fur monger flopped back in his seat, huffing and puffing, put the truck in gear and set off down the road.

Just as they entered Milo he pulled over. "Here is your money. That road will take you back to Bangor. From there you can find your way anywhere."

"Thank you said Busta," Handing some of the money back to the man. "For your trouble."

"Trouble? You ain't seen trouble. If they find out I helped you get out of town I will have trouble." The man sat there looking at Busta. "Keep your money. You're going to need it." And with that Busta got out of the truck, unloaded his pack and started down the road. The fur monger put his truck in gear and drove off. Neither man ever saw the other again.

That ain't the end of the story though. The next day Johnny woke up still wondering where Busta had gone off to that evening so he headed back there to see what happened after he left and to see if anyone knew where Busta was. Johnny walked in and sat at the bar.

"Little early for a drink Johnny isn't it?" The bartender, Al, asked.

"Well I'd have some breakfast if it suits ya," Johnny replied.

"Sure. And to drink?"

"Whatever is good," Johnny replied.
A couple minutes later Al came back.

"So, what happened after I left last night?" Johnny asked.

"Nothing," Al replied. "Guys had a few drinks and left. Why do you ask?"

"Just wondering if Busta ever came back and what Ray had in mind."

"Well if he had it wouldn't have been good. Think Ray and the guys would have got their message across," Al told him.

"That's what I thought. Any idea where Busta might be?"

"Well, that I might. Glad no one asked last night," Al paused. "Room 3. Upstairs"

"What? Really?" Johnny asked.

"I see what you guys pulled here last night. Good move," Al said. "I think I was the only one in the bar to see him leave."

"What?" Johnny said again. "You saw him leave and you didn't say anything?"

"I don't want my place all busted to hell. Al replied. I was glad he left. Damn fool caused enough problems with that bear and all."

"That is all Ray," Johnny said. "Anyone else see a hoof-ma-goof? No. Not even a sight of one. Ray just doesn't like flatlanders or people from away anywhere near him and Busta built a cabin straight across the cove up there on the lake. Now he can't go down to the water and take a piss in the morning without seeing Busta doing the same."
Al laughed. "Guess you're right Johnny."

"You haven't seen him this morning, have you?" Johnny asked.

"No but it is time for him to be up and out." Al hollered out back, "Sue! Go clean out room 3 and tell him he has someone down here that wants to see him."

About five minutes later Sue came in from the back. "He's gone. Never stayed in the room. Just left this." She handed Al the letter.

"It's for you," Al said as he handed the letter to Johnny.

"Well I wonder what this is."

Johnny opened the letter and read it sitting there at the bar while Al and Sue went back to work. After Johnny finished reading it he just shook his head. Al noticed Johnny had finished the letter and continued to just sit there. He had a lost and dumbfounded look on his face. "What did it say?" Al asked.

"It said his gun is at the town office."

"What?"

"He's gone. Said he got a letter that his folks needed help, that his dad was sick and he left." Johnny handed the letter to Al. As Al read it he said, "Sounds funny to me. I think he just got scared. Says here he left the cabin to you also. Maybe you ought to go get that gun. Seems that hoof-ma-goof might not be just in Ray's head after all, huh?"

"Yeah maybe not."

"So, what are you going to do?" Al asked.

"Well," Johnny said, "I figure I go get that rifle then pack up some things and go check out that cabin."

As Johnny got up to leave Al said, "Good luck...and watch yourself."

"Thanks," Johnny said as he left. He made his way down to the town office. The clerk there gave him a hard time stating that she couldn't give the gun to just anyone. Johnny showed her the letter but she was still reluctant. An officer hanging up posters overheard the conversation and came over. "Hey, can you talk to her?" Johnny asked.

"What's the problem?" He asked.

"Well my friend had to leave his rifle here yesterday. I'm trying to pick it up and she won't hand it over." Johnny handed the letter to the officer.

"I know this man," The officer said, looking at the clerk. "He's no thief. Let him have the rifle."

As the clerk was getting it the officer asked, "What's a hoof-ma-goof?"

"Just a bear," Johnny replied. "Just a bear."

"Good luck," The officer said. He shook Johnny's hand and went about his business.

"Here you go sir," She said as she handed it through the window. Johnny took the rifle and headed home.

When he got there, he sat in his room and looked around then started packing. He only grabbed a few things; some clothes, blankets and supplies, then he headed for the lake stopping at the general store for food, bullets and fuel for the lamps. It was around noon as he headed up the lake road. With his bad leg he knew it would be a long trip but he still thought he could make it before dark. Johnny had just gotten out of sight of town and he could hear a truck coming his way. It was Paul with another load of goods for the dam.

Chapter Seven
The Cabin

"Need a ride?" He asked.

"Sure do. I'm headed for the lake to check on a camp," Johnny said as he climbed in. "A friend had to leave and go help out his folks and left me his cabin."

"How'd that guy up there ever make out with that bear?" Paul asked.

"What? What guy?" Johnny asked.

"Didn't know him. Trapper from away. Said he had a bear problem. I gave him a ride to town and back up to the lake a while ago. Never heard anything again."

"Busta," Johnny said.

"Busta," Paul repeated. "Ya, that was his name. He ever get that bear?"

"Not so sure," Johnny said. "It's his cabin I'm headed to."

"Well I'd be careful. He was all shook up over it."

Johnny just stared at Paul and then turned and looked out the window. Neither man said much after that. When they reached the lake, Johnny got out and thanked Paul for the ride, grabbed his gear and started down the path to the cabin. He still had plenty of daylight left for the walk. As Johnny got closer to the cabin, he began to get uneasy. He stopped to make sure the rifle he was carrying was loaded. It was. "Why you letting yourself get all worked up?" He said to himself. "Just a bear. See him, shoot him." On down the path he went not stopping again until he reached the cabin. Johnny walked in to the clearing slowly looking all around, checking everything out, making sure there wasn't anything there waiting for him. He made his way to the front door and as he made his way up the stairs, he noticed claw marks on the door but it was still shut. "Old," He said softly. "They're old." But that didn't make him drop his guard. With one finger on the trigger he slowly opened the door. Everything was in its place right where Busta had left it. Johnny went inside and locked the door behind him.

First things first, he thought; let's get a fire going. In no time at all Johnny had the cabin all warmed up. As he began unloading his pack and putting things away, he began to notice claw marks and teeth marks inside the cabin. Some on the table and chairs, some on the floor, some on the pots and pans. At first Johnny didn't know what to think of all these marks and dents. He looked around and then it hit him. That bear. That bear had been in the cabin but Busta had never told me that and Paul didn't mention it and neither did Ray. What have I got myself in to Johnny was thinking as he stood there looking? The longer he looked the more he saw.

Finally, Johnny snapped out of it. He got the lantern lit and finished loading the stove one more time. Then he laid down keeping the rifle by his side the whole time. I'll talk to Ray tomorrow he thought, and make things right. Johnny blew out the lantern and drifted off to sleep.

The next morning the sun beamed through the window and as Johnny woke, he barely knew where he was. Looking around he thought he was still in a dream. Laying there taking it all in, this is mine, he thought. A place of my own. Whatever it takes I'm staying right here. No more town life. No more.

Johnny got up and made his way outside with rifle in hand. It had snowed that night about an inch or so. It made everything calm and white. A little slippery walking to the outhouse but still peaceful.

Coming out he looked around for tracks of a bear but found none. Johnny walked down to the lake and looked over towards Rays place. There he was pissing in the lake. Well ain't that a sight he thought. Johnny let him finish before he hollered out. "Ray! We need to talk!"

"Said all I need to!" Ray hollered back.

"It's John, Ray. And we need to talk. I'll put the coffee on."

Ray waved his hand and Johnny went back to the cabin. A few minutes later Johnny heard a boat land on the shore. The unmistakable sound of a metal boat on the rocks. That meant Ray was here. He walked over and opened the door. Ray was tying the boat off.

"Coffee is hot," Johnny said.

Johnny left the door open and went and sat at the table. As Ray got to the door Johnny said, "Come on in. Just you and me here. Pour yourself a cup and sit a spell. We need to talk. For starters, what the hell is going on up here?" Johnny said. "Busta's done gone and left me the cabin. You done scared him right out of here. I get here and see this place all chewed up. Claw marks all over the place, inside and out."

"What do you mean Busta's gone?" Ray asked.

"Left me this letter the other night. Said his folks needed him." Johnny handed Ray the letter. Ray sat there and read it. Johnny didn't say a word but when Ray looked up and set the letter down, Johnny looked him straight in the face and asked, "What's going on? No b.s.. Start at the beginning because I don't know what is going on. Why would Busta leave and leave me his cabin?"

Ray looked at Johnny and sat back in his chair. "How long have we known each other? Eight, ten years?"

"Ya about that," Johnny answered.

"Ok then. So, you know what? I say it's the truth!" Ray slammed down his hand on the table.

"Ya," Johnny said. "I never knew you to lie."

Ray started telling Johnny about Busta checking the bear in that oversized trap. The awful ruckus it made that night. The encounter with Busta the next day and what he had seen. The bears foot laying on the stump. The mess it had made of his canoe and cabin. Then Ray sat back in the chair, took a sip of coffee, and said, "Now Busta slips away and leaves."

"Well..." Johnny started.

Ray interrupted, "Well shit. He left you here to deal with this bear. A hoof-ma-goof. You know what's going to happen next spring, don't you? If no one kills it before winter sets in."

"Yea," Johnny said with a heavy load on his mind, "Yes I do. Nothing on this side of the lake will be safe."

"You got that right," Ray said. "That's what I kept telling Busta but he didn't want to hear it. Damn flatlander thinks he knows what the hell is going on. He don't know crap. And now he leaves you here. Don't go anywhere without that gun and if you see the damn thing put a bullet in it."

"Well I wish I would have known what was going on. I just thought you two had a tiff. If I had known about all this, I would have tried to get him to stay," Johnny said.

"Well it's a little late for that," Ray replied as he finished his coffee. "So, what you going to do now? You going to stay up or head back to town?"

Johnny looked at Ray and said, "Well he left it to me and if you don't mind having me as a neighbor, I think I might stay right up here."

"Don't mind at all," Ray told him.

"I will have to make a couple trips in to town, get the rest of my things and some supplies," Johnny said, hunting for a ride.

"I'll be headed that way in a couple of days if you can wait."

"Oh yea. I got enough for a couple days. Sure, would appreciate it," Johnny said as he stood up holding his hand out.

"Ok," Ray said, shaking Johnny's hand. "I'll see you in the morning, day after tomorrow." Ray turned back and looked at Johnny as he made his way to the door. "I meant what I said. Keep that rifle handy. Any problems I'm not that far away. Just keep shooting. I'll hear ya."

"Ya, thanks," Johnny said. They walked outside and Ray looked around. "Sure, did bust the place, up didn't he?"

"Not too bad," Johnny answered. "But you sure know he was here."

"Well I'm gonna get so I'll see you later," Ray said as he climbed in to his boat. "And like I said, just holler if you need help."

"Thanks Ray," Johnny replied as he pushed the little boat out in the lake, "But I'm sure I'll be just fine."

Ray gave a pull on the little two horse outboard and she fired right up. Backing out into the lake he gave a wave then put it in gear and off he went back across the cove.

A cold gust of wind hit Johnny as he turned around making him stop and think, winter is coming and it won't be long until it is here. "Well I guess I need to check things out a little more closely," Johnny said to no one but himself. He went back into the cabin but only to get the rifle. I'll have plenty of time to check out the inside tonight he thought to himself as he went back outside. Johnny checked out the wood supply and climbed up to check out the stash box; not much stacked in it though. He saw the canoe while climbing down the ladder and went to look at it. "Wow," He whispered, looking at the hole Busta fixed and the claw marks on its side and bottom. That bear was mad. He was right there and no time like the present. The outhouse was only a few steps away and nature was calling. Yup, door works fine, seat is clean, and the hole ain't full. That's about as good as it gets as far as outhouses go. After he finished up there, he walked around checking the outside of the cabin looking for tracks in what was left of the snow but not finding anything.

Johnny only brought a little food with him but there was a big lake right there in front of him so he went and got the pole Busta had left. It took a while to find something for bait. Under an old log by the firewood pile Johnny finally found a night crawler. He threaded it on the hook but only half of it, saving the other half in case the fish were biting. He had made a good cast then propped up the pole so a big fish wouldn't drag it out in the lake. After that Johnny went back to looking around. He had plenty to do. Loading up the wood box would be first on the list. In and out of the cabin he went, checking his pole each time. Johnny didn't like where Busta had left the canoe so he dragged it to the sheltered side of the cabin. When Ray drove him in to town, he would pick up some nails to make a rack so it would be off the ground for the winter.

About that time Johnny noticed the pole bouncing all over so he went running over. A nice white perch was on the line but his bait was gone. Good thing he only used half of that crawler. With the hook re-baited and the pole cast back out, Johnny waited for a minute hoping for another bite but no luck so back at it he went. In and out of the cabin checking food and pots and pans and all that was left so he could make a list for town.

The only thing Johnny kept walking around was the set right there in the yard where the bear had lost its foot. That's gotta go he thought and started to move it one piece at a time. Busta had an outside fire pit and that's right where it was all going. Piece by piece Johnny dragged and carried the whole set to the fire pit. When he was just about

73

half way finished he got a fire going and by the time the last log made it to the pit the fire was roaring. All the while he kept his eye on the pole. Johnny had stopped to enjoy the fire and quiet of the day when he noticed the pole bent right over. "Oh gee!" He exclaimed and started running. Just as he got to the pole the line went slack. "Shit!" Johnny exclaimed as he grabbed the pole and started reeling it in. Tug, tug, tug. The fish was still on the line. "Oh nice one," Johnny said as he continued to reel. Another nice perch. "Nice," Johnny repeated. "These two will make a great suppa."

There was still enough daylight so he cleaned both the fish and loaded the rest of the set on the fire pit. Johnny went in to the cabin and grabbed a potato. He put a stick through it and placed it next to the fire. Baked 'tater and perch. What a supper tonight. He thought he could get used to this. As the fire died down, he put the fish on a rack and inched it toward the fire. Not too close to burn but not so far away that it wouldn't cook. The smell of fresh perch filled the air. A half hour later Johnny was thinking it couldn't get much better than this. A good plate full of perch and potato. The sun setting behind him, Johnny loaded the last of the set on the fire then sat back to eat his meal and enjoyed life.

The night started to get cool but the fire was warm. Loons on the lake were laughing at one another. The fire was popping from the spruce and fir. Johnny never gave it a thought as he threw the scraps of perch in the fire but not out in the middle where the fire was going strong. No, right on the edge of the pit. The smell of perch once again filled the air. By now the fire was not much of a fire, just a couple of small flames and a lot of hot coals. Johnny took his plate and headed for the cabin. He put his plate in the sink and got the oil lantern lit. It hadn't taken very long and it was dark outside. There was still some light from the fire when Johnny made his way to the outhouse with oil lamp in hand. Sitting there with his pants around his ankles when the fire went black and then it showed through the cracks once more. Johnny sat there still trying not to make a sound as he listened intently. Pop, pop, pop...grunt, pop, pop. It had been a long time but Johnny knew just what the sound was. The bear was back. Popping his jaw, tasting the air and looking for food. Did I leave the door to the cabin open, he wondered? No, I don't think so but I did leave the rifle in it. How stupid can I get? I left the gun in the cabin he thought to himself. Really? Really? Johnny sat there in disbelief. Now what the hell am I going to do? Peeking through the cracks Johnny watched the bear circle the fire. He could see it was the hoof-ma-goof. The bear ate what was left of the perch then started looking around for more. It made its way to the cabin steps. Oh no you don't, Johnny thought. He turned up the lantern to get a full glow then kicked the door open. "Get outta here!" Johnny yelled. The bear was startled and ran around the back side of the cabin. Johnny finished up in the outhouse and headed for the cabin. Looking everywhere in the dark while quickly making his way closing and locking the door behind him. Johnny took a deep breath. Don't want to do that again he thought.

On the way in to town the next day Johnny told Ray about his visitor. Ray kind of chuckled when he heard the bear caught Johnny with his pants down, literally. When they got to town Ray dropped Johnny off at his room and said he would be back in a couple hours to help load his belongings. When he did show back up Johnny had everything waiting. It didn't take long to load the truck. After one stop at the market for supplies they were back on the road. The two men made their way to Ray's house. They loaded all Johnny's things in Rays boat and after two trips across the the cove Johnny had all his belongings at the cabin. Rays wife had made a good supper for them and by the time they finished eating it was dark. Ray knew the cove well and had no problem taking Johnny back to his cabin even in the dark. The air was cold and the men could see their breath.

"It won't be long and she'll be all frozen over." Ray said. He guided the boat slowly to the beach. "Keep your gun handy. That bear may still come back."

Johnny got out of the boat. "It won't be too long and it should be hibernating right?"

"Yeah, not too long," Ray replied.

"Thanks for everything," Johnny said as he pushed the boat back out into the lake. "And tell your wife supper was great. You're a lucky man Ray."

Johnny made his way into the cabin and Ray made his way across the cove. Johnny got a fire going to warm up his new place then he started putting things away. Around midnight he opened up the front door and stepped out on to the porch. It was snowing again, a light, fluffy snow. It was as calm and peaceful as it could get. Johnny stood there a minute or so just to let it all sink in then turned and went back inside. He loaded up the stove one more time then retired for the night.

When Johnny awoke the next morning, it was still snowing but it had changed to a fine light snow and it was starting to pile up. Eight inches in all fell that night then more came two days later. The cove froze over not long after that. Johnny never had another issue with the hoof-ma-goof that fall. Winter set in quickly.

When the ice was safe to walk on and the days were sunny, Johnny would try to catch some fish and when he had a real good day on the ice, he would go visit Ray and his wife. He also took some of Busta's traps and made his way to the beaver dam on Grant Brook. Fresh beaver in the middle of winter, now that was a good meal. Some rabbit here and there also made it on the menu. By the time the snow was three feet deep and no end in sight, Johnny was wondering what he had gotten himself in to. But then as quick as winter had set in, it was gone. The snow started to disappear just as Johnny had gotten to the last tier of wood in the pile.

Spring came on quick and Johnny had a sense of pride. Even with his bad leg he made it through the winter up here by himself. One day after the ice went out in the cove Johnny could hear Ray's boat coming. Johnny met him on the shore.

"Full moon coming up Johnny in a couple of days," Ray said. "Going to be heading to Sandy and get a mess of smelts if you want to come along."

"Oh ya. Thanks for the invite," Johnny said, "I got some coffee on. Come on in."

"No," Ray said. "Just testing out the mortar before the trip but thanks. See you in a couple days."

"Sounds good," Johnny said and pushed Ray back out in the lake. He stood there and watched Ray take the boat through its paces.

The full moon was up and it was still daylight when Ray picked up Johnny and they headed across the lake. When they reached Sandy Stream the water was running black with smelts.

"Looks like you called that one right," Johnny said as they began filling their nets. After filling

77

three buckets they headed back across the lake. It was just getting dark when they got back to Johnny's cabin. "Thanks Ray. This is going to make a good suppa."

"Yea I need to drop off half of these to the neighbors tonight. Some people just can't go anymore you know."

"Thanks again," Johnny repeated.

Ray nodded, "I'll see you later," he said then headed for the cove.

"Well I've got some work to do," Johnny said as he looked at the bucket of little fish and off to the cabin he went. Dumping the fish in the sink he realized how many he had. The sink was three inches deep with them. I'm never going to be able to eat all of these before they go bad, he thought. That didn't matter now though. Johnny got out his little knife and cutting board and started in. He had them about half cleaned before he started supper. Not much beats a good mess of smelts early in the year. He kept cleaning right up until they were finished cooking then he sat down to eat. A little salt and pepper and they were good as gone. "That tasted like another one," he said and got up and cooked another frying pan full. In no time that one was also gone. That was enough. The rest could wait until the morning. The ones he had cleaned he put in mason jars and set them in the ice chest then he dumped a gallon of water in the sink. This would help keep them fresh. Johnny didn't want to waste the other parts of the fish so he put those in mason jars as well. This he would let render down for a good trapping bait. After setting them on the porch he retired to bed.

The next morning Johnny got a fire going outside in the pit early in the morning then he filled a dutch oven full of beans and water to soak. These would be a good addition to the smelts for supper tonight. After getting the beans ready he went back to cleaning the rest of the smelts. Five more quarts. Seven in all. "I'll have just one more tonight," He said to himself.

Watching the beans cook and enjoying the afternoon Johnny thought to himself, I might as well make some jerky out of those little buggers. They will last longer that way. Off to work he went. A rack, a teepee, a little wire here and there you go. He laid the little fish out to dry. Add some fresh alder for smoke flavor and wait.

The beans were done just about dark. He was working on the second batch of jerky when he went in the cabin for supper. The smell of fish filled the air. After eating and taking care of the dishes Johnny walked down to check on how his smoked jerky was coming along. Should be just about done, he thought.

Chapter Eight
The Fire

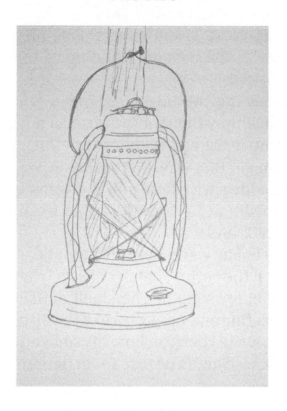

It was a beautiful night and quiet. Johnny could see camp fires across the cove and he knew everyone was enjoying it as much as he was. He tried one of the smelts. Just about there but he was out of wood. With the old oil lamp in hand Johnny went to fetch some more. As he picked up his first piece of wood from the pile the hoof-ma-goof stood up on his hind legs not more than ten feet away right on the other side of the wood pile. Johnny, startled and scared as hell, started to back up but with his bad leg he tripped, landing flat on his back. The oil lamp landed right on his chest and broke. Johnny was on fire. He started screaming at the top of his lungs rolling around in the dirt but he had just filled the oil lamp and with that much oil the fire wouldn't go out. He jumped up and ran, one great big ball of fire, in to the lake.

Ray and his neighbor were a couple of the people out enjoying this peaceful evening when the see Johnny on fire, screaming and running for the lake. Ray just started running for his boat. Kermit, Ray's neighbor, right on his heels. Ray dove to the back of the boat and with one pull the little motor started up. Kermit pushed the boat in three feet of water before jumping in.

"That ain't good," Kermit said.

"Not good at all," Ray replied.

When they got to Johnny, he was floating on his back still smoking. Both men thought he was dead. Then Johnny took a deep breath and screamed, "Bear!" before blacking out again.

"We gotta get him to town," Ray said as Kermit jumped out of the boat. The men carefully got Johnny in to the boat and started back across the cove.

"Start the truck! Start the truck!" Ray hollered to his wife. When they reached Ray's beach other neighbors were there to help them get Johnny out of the boat and in to the back of the truck. They wrapped him in blankets the best they could then off to Millinocket they went. Kermit sat in the back of the truck with Johnny bundled up between his legs and his head on his lap.

"Just keep breathing Johnny. Just keep breathing," Kermit repeated over and over.

The two men got Johnny to the hospital still alive. There was nothing more they could do. It would be up to the nurses, doctors and Johnny now. The hospital staff told Kermit and Ray to just go home and pray. You did all you could do, now let us do our job.

"You see his face?" Kermit asked Ray as they were getting in to the truck.

"Yea," Ray replied. "He'll never be the same."

"Ya, he is burned bad. I wonder what the hell happened."

Ray looked at Kermit and said, "I don't know but, in the morning, I am going to find out."

Kermit and Ray climbed back in the truck and headed north. It was a very somber ride and the men didn't talk. Once they reached Ray's driveway Kermit said, "I'd like to go over there with you," meaning Johnny's place, "If you don't mind. Help you figure this out."

"Thank you," Ray said. "I'll give you a holler."

"Don't think I'll get much sleep tonight," Kermit replied.

"Me either," Answered Ray.

Kermit turned away and walked through the woods back to his house. It seemed every light was on in both Ray and Kermits' home. Their wives were waiting for word of how Johnny was.

The next day after coffee, Ray hollered to Kermit. Both men met at the boat and headed for Johnny's cabin. They landed at the beach. The smell of fire was still in the air and the fire pit was still smoldering. Ray and Kermit started to look around. Kermit stopped at the fire pit and Ray kept walking looking for what could have turned Johnny in to a human torch. It didn't take but five more steps before Ray saw what he was looking for. A charred, burned, black circle over by the wood pile. Ray headed straight for it. He stood there replaying what had happened. It was a miracle the whole place hadn't gone up in flames. The old oil lamp lay broken next to a couple pieces of firewood. Just a few of the pine needles on the ground were burnt.

"Happened over here," Ray said, "But something ain't right."

Kermit walked over.

"Looks like he was getting wood for the fire but look at the scuff marks. He was walking backwards, tripped, then all hell broke loose. Near as I can tell by the fire pit, he had a teepee with a rack under it cooking fish."

"Smelts," said Kermit, "We went the other night. He was making jerky. You see any on the rack?"

"Nope," The rack was on the ground and the teepee was laying on top of it. Ray turned to look at the cabin and started walking to the door. He noticed three broken mason jars at the bottom of the steps. He bent over and picked up the lid of one of them. It had teeth marks on it. Holes punched right through it. "Johnny was putting up bait," Ray said, "And that ain't no coon that did that. It's that damned hoof-ma-goof. That explains why Johnny said bear."

"Wait. What?" Asked Kermit.

"Busta created one, the guy that gave Johnny the cabin. He got scared and left in the middle of the night. Johnny moved in and had a run in with it last fall just before the snow came. Last week the damned thing showed back up. I bet Johnny cooking those fish out here called him right back. It caught Johnny off guard while he was getting wood. That's why he was walking backwards and fell."

"Whoa, whoa, whoa," Kermit said with kind of a chuckle. "Busta created a hoof-ma-goof and that's what caused Johnny to catch on fire? You're joking right? Ray"

"This shit ain't over until the hoof-ma-goof dies," Ray said, looking Kermit straight in the eyes as he walked past him and headed for the boat. "If you want a ride back home you better get in the boat. Or you can wait for him to come back and then tell me I'm crazy."

"You keep the doors locked and the guns loaded and close by you," Ray told his wife before he drove in to town that afternoon. He stopped by the hospital to see how Johnny was doing. The nurse told him they had sent him to Bangor and then maybe to Portland. He was stable when he left but she had not heard how he was doing since. She would try to find out
more and stop by but he wouldn't be home for some time.

"He is lucky you were there," she said, "He might not be alive otherwise."

Ray walked out and headed to the tavern. He figured he would get the message out about Johnny and the hoof-ma-goof. Ray walked in to the tavern and settled up at the bar. There were only a few people in there at that time. Al came over. "What'll you have?" he asked.

"Oh just a beer I guess. You hear about Johnny?"

"No. What do you mean? What about Johnny?"

"Well I told you all about Busta and that hoof-ma-goof. Well it got Johnny."

"What? What happened?"

Ray took a drink of his beer then told Al about the fire and the smelts and how everything looked at the cabin.

"Maybe he just tripped Ray," suggested Al.

"Then the lantern wouldn't have landed on him, he would have landed on it," Ray snapped. "When we got to him, he said one word. Bear. Then he passed back out from the pain. I'm not crazy and this stuff is going to keep happening until that bear is killed. Mark my words. No one around the lake is safe. You let people know."

"Yea ok Ray."

By this time all the people in the bar were listening to Ray.

"Sorry to hear about Johnny," Al said. "The drink is on the house for what you did and I will let people know."

Ray finished his beer and left. As he drove the old truck back home, he could smell Johnny's burnt skin and clothes. It was a quiet ride but Ray could hear Johnny scream bear over and over. Even as he lay down to bed, he could hear Johnny scream.

Chapter Nine
The Summer of the Hoof-ma-goof

As the days went by things got better and Johnny didn't haunt Ray so much. Then one night, it might have been a week or so after the accident, Ray heard three gunshots from across the lake.

At sunrise Ray headed across to Sandy Stream where they had dipped smelts. As he got closer, he could see smoke and a tent. Ray pulled up his boat and hollered, "Everything okay here?"

A young man came out of the tent. "Yeah, all good this morning. Had a bear last night though."

"That you that fired the gun last night?" Ray asked.

"Yeah, I took a shot at him. Why?"

"You kill it?"

"No. I don't know though. It ran off kind of funny though like I hit it. I looked a little bit ago and didn't see any blood. I'm not sure."

Ray looked at the young man and said, "It ran off on three legs and it will be back. If I were you, I would be getting the hell out of here."

The young man scoffed at Ray and said, "I ain't afraid of no bear."

"It's a hoof-ma-goof and he knows there is food here so he will be back."

"I will be waiting," said the young man. "Thanks for the warning old timer."

That made Ray mad. "Don't say you weren't warned. It's not safe here." With that Ray headed for home.

Ray was lying in bed that night when he thought he heard two more gunshots echo across the lake, although it could have been anything.

In the morning curiosity got the better of him. He went next door to ask Kermit if he had heard the gunshots the two previous nights. He had. Kermit got his rifle after Ray told him about the young man on Sandy Point. "We ought to go check on him," Kermit said.

Ray agreed. "I'll meet you at the boat. I'm getting mine too." Pointing at Kermit's rifle.

The two men took the boat across the lake. When they got there, it was a different scene than before. Smoke was still coming from the fire pit but that was the only thing the same. The tent was shredded and things were scattered all over the place. Kermit and Ray started hollering in an attempt to find the young man.

"Hello! Hello! Anyone here?"

They walked around and cased out what had happened and tried to find the young man. Alive or dead. After an hour or so and a stomp through the woods the men were in agreement. No blood, no bear, no rifle, no young man, and no boat or canoe. But the bear had been there. They left the area as they had found it and got back in to the boat. They had just rounded the point when Kermit saw someone in a canoe paddling their way from Mud Brook.

"Think we ought to let him know?" Kermit asked, pointing at the canoe. Ray nodded and turned the boat around. It was the cocky young man all by himself paddling into the wind trying to get back to sandy point. Ray pulled up beside him.

"Boy am I glad to see you again. I should have listened to you. I'm sorry for not taking your advice. I should have left just as soon as you did yesterday."

"What happened?" Kermit asked.

"That thing. Whatever you call it. It came right through my tent wall. I touched off the rifle then backed it off, but only for a minute. I ran for my canoe and shot it off again while I was running from it. I got to the canoe and started paddling. I fell asleep on the lake and woke up down in Mud Cove. I guess your boat woke me up. Been paddling a while now but not making much headway. Could I have a tow to the point?"

Ray tossed the young man a rope and towed him back to Sandy Point.

"Thanks again. I didn't get your name sir."

"Ray," he replied.

"Ray," The young man repeated. "Well Ray, you were right. I should have left. Sorry I didn't listen. You were right about another thing too. It was missing one foot. A front one."

Ray just looked at Kermit.

"What did you call it?" The young man asked.

"It's a Hoof-ma-goof. Tell people to stay away from here, you understand? It won't be safe until it is dead."

"Oh yes sir. I'm going to get my stuff and go home. Not coming back here!" The young man said shaking his head. "Thanks again Ray. And you too mister, thanks." The young man paddled for shore.

Kermit and Ray headed home. Nothing was said the whole ride. When they landed the boat at Ray's place Kermit looked at Ray and said, "That kid got lucky."

Ray nodded his head. "But how many more will be? This isn't over. Summer just started."

All that summer people kept running into the hoof-ma-goof. Some on Sandy Stream and some on Mud Brook. Some said they saw him at Omaha Beach and others at Abol campground. Five got a shot off. Some said they hit or wounded him but someone somewhere days later would have a run in with him.

Ray kept up on Johnny's recovery. They did send him to Boston. In Johnny's condition that is where he needed to be. Ray also kept notes on where people said they had an encounter with the hoof-ma-goof. He was trying to follow him over the summer.

As fall rolled around Ray got word that Johnny was going to be coming home. Ray was surprised by this but he received a letter from Johnny.

To my friend Ray,

I can't put into words what the past months have been like but I am alive and doing okay. They work with me every day getting my mobility back. I don't like it here. I need to get back to Maine and the lake. It is so peaceful there. It is going to be a long road for me but I have plenty of time.
They say I'll be able to leave here the last week of September. Was hoping I could ask you to pick me up in Bangor and get me home.
I'll stay in touch.

Johnny

Ray knew what needed to be done at Busta's, at Johnny's cabin just to get through the winter but he couldn't do it alone. Ray went and told Kermit that Johnny was coming home. Kermit couldn't believe his ears.

"Ray," he said. "He got no wood. No food stashed. No supplies. What is he thinking? He ought to just stay in town the winter even if he wants to be up here.

"I know," Ray said. "That's why I am here. People know Johnny and a lot of them say, if I can do anything just let me know."

Ray drove in to town with Kermit in the passenger's seat. They went place to place letting people know what was up. Then, on the second Saturday in September, people by the droves pulled in to Ray's dooryard. Some with food, some with dry goods, then some with nothing but their hands, but all willing to help.

Ray gave up trying to get everyone from his place to Johnny's and handed his boat to the young man that him and Kermit had pulled from Mud Brook.

Hand saws and axes were in heavy use. The one thing Ray was consumed with was the wood pile. Food could be found but getting enough wood for the winter can take all summer. But with the help of twenty men, Ray couldn't believe what happened. All the winters supply was cut to length and stacked in just two days. People didn't leave when it got dark that first day. Rather they brought bed rolls and camped out at Johnny's. One man stayed up and fed the fire with a gun close at hand. No sign of the hoof-ma-goof that night.

The weekend passed with no issues. Enough wood was cut and piled for even the longest of winters. There was more food in the cabin than had ever been there before. Johnny was all set up for the winter.

As all the men worked and talked that weekend, Ray had heard about six different cabins and camps that had been broken into and raided over the summer by a bear. No one could be certain if it was the hoof-ma-goof or just a bear. One thing they all agreed on was that this wouldn't happen next year. All trappers and loggers alike would have a rifle on them until the hoof-ma-goof was found dead.

Ray thanked each and every man that came to help that weekend. As they left, he wondered how he could ever repay the debt. Kermit was standing there with Ray when the last man got in his truck to leave.

"I can't believe how many men came," Ray said in disbelief.

"They all came because of you Ray. Just goes to show when a good man asks for help, he gets it."

Kermit left for home and Ray went inside to his wife for supper.

Ray got up every morning and made his way across the cove just to make sure everything was still there and the hoof-ma-goof had not broken in. Ray felt responsible for everything at the cabin. So many people had helped.

Trapping season was fast approaching and Ray decided to follow Busta's trap line to the lean to and back. Maybe he could do what Busta didn't and kill the hoof-ma-goof. So, one morning, with rifle in hand, Ray set off to remark and open back up Busta's trap line to his lean to. Ray was kind of impressed by what he saw. How well it was marked and where the traps were set. Although most of the cubbies were destroyed Ray could see where they were and quickly figured it was the work of the hoof-ma-goof. He rebuilt each one but did not bait them. That would come later.

He reached the lean to around lunch and was glad to see that it was still standing and in good condition. He would bring supplies by boat before trapping started. The wood pile he was most pleased with. Busta had left it in good shape.

Ray didn't stay there long. Just long enough to check things out then he headed back to the cabin, moving down trees as he had to and occasionally marking trees where need be. Ray made it back to the cabin and back to his house around dark.

Chapter Ten
Johnny Came Home

The next couple of weeks flew by. Ray finally received another letter. Johnny would be in Bangor on the third of October. Ray would be there to drive him home.

Ray spotted Johnny right off quick at quite some distance. Ray watched him not knowing what to say or how to act. Johnny had a big scarf around his neck covering most of his face. He was walking with the use of a cane. His leg looked to be a little worse than before the accident. Ray stood up and hollered, "Johnny!" and waved his hand. Johnny waved back.

"I could use a little help with my bag Ray, if you don't mind."

"No, not at all," Ray said. "Not at all. I'm parked over here."

Ray helped Johnny in the truck. "It's going to be a long ride home. If you need me to stop just let me know."

"No. I'll be fine. Might fall asleep on you though."

"If you do, I'm going to hit a pothole," Ray said, and both men chuckled.

Ray wasn't five minutes down the road before Johnny fell asleep. Ray let him sleep. He knew it must have been a long trip up from Boston. As he drove, he kept looking over to check on Johnny. The scarf he had wrapped around his face and neck slowly slid down revealing what the fire had done. Johnny's face had got burned pretty bad. Ray could see scars up and down his cheek from ear to his throat. Ray tried not to stare.

By the time they reached Millinocket Ray could see the whole side of Johnny's face. The scars were terrible. He was missing part of his bottom lip and drool was running down his chin. Ray couldn't believe how bad the damage was. He had never seen someone burned before.

Johnny woke up and realized the scarf was no longer covering his face. He sat there a minute to see Ray's reaction. Ray kept driving and looking over occasionally. At one point he saw that Johnny was awake but pretending to be asleep so he hit a pothole. Johnny started to giggle and Ray laughed.

"Well," Johnny said, wiping the drool off his chin, "Your driving hasn't improved while I was away."

"Neither did your looks," Ray said. Too soon he thought and waited.

"Go to hell Ray!" Johnny snapped back then laughed after a brief pause. Ray was slightly relieved.

"Well," he said, "I know I look like hell but for the most part I am okay. Just look like crap. Not going to win any beauty contests, that's for sure. Took a long time for me to come around. I'm not dead, just lost some skin. I laid in bed so long I had to learn to walk again," Johnny kept talking and Ray kept listening. "They know their stuff down there in Boston. They made me work every day to get my strength back. Stretches every morning or I would tighten up at night. Lost some movement in my left hand. Fingers don't all work right, but they said that would come back eventually. My chest got it pretty bad; back of my neck too. Doctors said it was from me running. It fanned the flames."

All the time Johnny was talking he kept sucking his saliva back up in to his mouth.

Slurp...slurp. "The only thing that gets to me is that I can't whistle anymore."

Ray choked back a laugh.

"They said it got infected and had to cut some of it off or it would have spread. For now, I am stuck like this. They might be able to fix it later but I wasn't going to spend the winter down there. I got a lot of work to do to stay at my place before winter comes," Johnny said.

"You think so?" Ray replied.

Johnny looked at Ray. "It's still there, right? It didn't burn down too did it? That damn hoof-ma-goof busted it all up. Well say something will ya!"

"Well Johnny," Ray began, "Let's just say you're staying at my house tonight."

"What the hell. You're not going to tell me about my own place?"

"No. I will just give you a ride over in the morning," Ray said as they turned in to the yard.

Johnny covered up his face and both men went inside.

"I would just as soon go to bed Ray. Don't want your wife seeing me this late. Might give her nightmares. I'll give you time to talk to her."

"Yeah, okay," Said Ray. "Bed is all made up for you. First door on the left, down the hall."

"Thanks for everything Ray," Johnny said as he limped down the hall.

Ray turned to his wife who was in the kitchen. He stood there with a look on his face she had never seen. It was a look of sadness and loss. He walked into the kitchen and held her close. For a long time, he didn't move. He wanted to remember everything at this moment. Slowly he started to tell her how badly Johnny was burned.

In the morning Ray and Johnny walked down to the boat. Johnny had a little trouble getting in but Ray kind of figured that beforehand. He razzed Johnny a little bit but not too much.

The little motor fired right up and they set off. It was a nice warm fall day.

"A good day for fishing," said Johnny as they crossed the cove.

"Yup," Ray answered, "Maybe we can go catch some perch tonight after you get settled."

"That would be some nice. Haven't had that in some time."

They hit the shore at Johnny's cabin. Johnny just looked at Ray. He shook his head then climbed out of the boat so Ray could join him. When Ray's feet hit the ground, Johnny gave him a backhand on his arm, "What did you do, spend all summer getting wood up for me?"

"No," said Ray. At least twenty men showed up last weekend and did that. Plus, some."

"What?" Johnny asked in disbelief, "What do you mean?"

"Well," Ray began, "Kermit and I went in to town to tell everyone that you were coming home and they all showed up last weekend. There's more than wood. Go take a look."

Johnny walked up to the cabin taking in all that had been done. Some wood by the fire pit ready to go. Five rows of wood for the winter, cut and piled next to the cabin so he wouldn't have to carry it. A nice pile in the wood shed too. The yard was all clean. Not what Johnny was expecting.

When he entered the house it still smelled clean, not like smoke or musty, but clean. Johnny stood there trying to remember how he had left it. It wasn't like this. Every shelf had food on it. Every cupboard was packed full. The bed was made and more blankets than he had ever had lay folded at one end. And yes, the wood box inside was full too. Johnny was overwhelmed. He walked to the table and sat down. Ray stepped inside and joined Johnny at the table.

"So," Ray said, "What do you think?"
Johnny, wiping tears back as he looked up, said, "Well, I can't believe my eyes. I never thought this would happen. All those traps hanging up there. I'd say they all smell like bleach, wouldn't you?"

Ray looked up, "Yup. I'd say so. I guess they left something for you to do after all."

Both men laughed. Johnny wanted to know who had been here and who had done what but Ray just said it was everyone that he had ever helped in the past. They all came to return the favor. The men talked for a while then Ray left for home leaving Johnny to get settled in.

A couple hours before dark Johnny heard Ray's little boat land on his rocky beach. Ray was good on his word. The wind was calm and the perch had to be hungry. Johnny had his pole handy and off he went.

As the two men were fishing Johnny asked Ray about the hoof-ma-goof. Did anyone get it or has anyone seen it? Ray broke the news to Johnny. It was still out there.

Now that bear toyed with Busta eating the baits out of his set and later eating the animals he would catch. After losing his foot it had to get smarter if it was going to survive. It did get smarter, but also bolder and it had a temper by the time Johnny returned home.

The night of the fire, as Johnny ran to the lake all ablaze, the bear watched from the blackness of the woods and after Kermit and Ray hauled Johnny off, he wandered around eating all the smelts he could find. It was an easy meal. The bear learned if he scared people, he would have free food, that simple. That is what he continued to do for a while.

Bears have a great nose. Trout on a fire is like ringing a dinner bell. When he would get to where someone was cooking and people were about, he would watch them from afar. Just back enough so not to be seen but close enough so he could learn. When the people either went to sleep or just left camp, it was a free for all. Coolers, backpacks, lunch boxes. Anything and everywhere they had stashed food were fair game to him. The more run-ins he had with people the braver and bolder he became, walking right out into the open during the day and right into campsites. Getting shot up at Sandy Stream one day though, taught him not to be quite so bold. The bullet had just grazed his back. Just enough to get his attention. He went back after dark and destroyed the camp site even though they shot him over and over. They never hit him again.

He finally started breaking into cabins eating anything edible and making a mess of anything that wasn't. No matter where he went anyone that saw him knew he was the hoof-ma-goof. Even if another bear had a run in with someone, the hoof-ma-goof got the blame.

He made it through the summer just fine while Johnny was in Boston dealing with the pain of being burned. Now that Johnny was home and Ray had given him an update, he knew it was only a matter of time. The hoof-ma-goof would make his rounds and find his way back to the cabin.

Ray told Johnny to keep his rifle on him at all times no matter what. "The bear will be back and you need to put a bullet in him."

The men fished for a while and the sun was setting.

"We better get back before it gets dark Ray."

"Yup. I was thinking the same thing," he replied.

The two men had caught plenty of fish for supper. Johnny asked Ray to take four of them over to Kermit's' place as a thank you for everything. Ray agreed and said he would bring him over so he could thank him in person but Johnny wanted to inform him of how he looked first. "I don't need to be scaring the life out of his wife or him or anyone. That's another reason why I came back here. The fewer people that see me the happier I will be."

Ray dropped Johnny off at his cabin and waited in the boat until he was on the porch before heading for home. After landing and tying up his boat Ray carried the string of perch into the house. He unstrung them in the sink and picked four of the biggest ones out to bring to Kermit.

It was just after dark when Ray knocked on the door. Kermit was surprised by the size of the perch Ray had handed him. The men talked briefly then Ray went home.

Kermit stopped by Ray's house the next day and Ray told him about how Johnny looked and how he wanted to thank him in person. Kermit agreed to go see him, so the two men hopped in Ray's little boat and made their way across the cove.

The timing couldn't have been worse. Johnny sat there eating the fresh perch at his table. When the two men knocked on his door Johnny was surprised. He had never heard the boat.

"Yeah," he hollered. Ray opened the door with Kermit right behind him.

"Got someone to see you," Ray said before he had even looked up. When he did, he was taken aback. Johnny was sitting there with no shirt on. Ray had seen his face but not the rest of him. The burns had left scars all over both arms and all of his chest. It looked as if his skin had melted; like wax from a candle. Little pieces of fish and oil covered his chin and chest. Saliva was running out of his mouth from where his bottom lip was missing and he couldn't wipe it fast enough.

With towel in hand, chewing what he had in his mouth, Johnny started wiping himself off. He jumped up and turned his back and quickly grabbed a shirt. Ray and Kermit turned their heads.

"Sorry Johnny," Ray said. "Didn't mean to catch you off guard."

"Too late for that now," Johnny replied as he put his shirt on and washed his face and hands.

"Kermit. He lives next to me," Ray said. "You told me you wanted to talk to him so I brought him over."

"Kermit," Johnny said. "Seen you around but never had the pleasure." Johnny limped over to the men. "I was told you jumped in and helped me to the boat that night. Got me all the way in to town with Ray here."

"Ya," Kermit answered.

"Well you seen me at my worse twice now," Sucking his saliva back in his mouth as he talked. Every few words and, slurp...slurp. "Don't really like people seeing me eat. You can understand that can't you?"

"Yes," Kermit said, "Sorry about that."

Johnny stuck out his hand and said, "I needed to tell you in person thank you. Thank you for helping Ray that night. I would probably be in a pine box right now if you two hadn't been there. It has been tough but I think I will get by, especially after all this. Never dream of all this."

Kermit gently shook Johnny's hand.

"Damned thing won't bite," Johnny told him as he gave him a firm shake back. "Thanks again. Anything I can do in return just let me know."

"I appreciate Johnny but I would have done it for anyone."

"Well whatever I can do," Johnny replied.

"Well Ray if you don't mind, I got to get back home. Glad you are okay Johnny. Oh, and thanks for the perch. Going to have them tonight for supper!"

"You're welcome. Stop in anytime. Just give a holler."

Kermit turned and left the cabin. Ray apologized again for just walking in on him while he was eating.

"Wasn't how I wanted to meet him but all is good. I said what I needed to say. I'd like to thank all the town folks for what they have done too but don't know how to do that."

Ray shook Johnny's hand and made his way to the boat. Kermit and Ray waved as they headed back across the cove. Johnny was still standing in the doorway of his cabin. He waved back then went inside.

Kermit was rattled by the whole experience.

"You warned me but still."

"I know." Ray replied.

Not another word was spoken on the trip back home.

Chapter 11
The Agreement

It was a week before Ray stopped in again. This time, he made plenty of noise getting out of the boat. Johnny came out of the cabin.

"Didn't think you were going to stop back in after last time," Johnny said.

Ray laughed, "I've seen a lot worse things than you eating. Hey, I was going to restock the lean to over at Sandy. Wondered if you wanted to go."

"Hell yeah. Let me get my boots on. I'll be just a minute," Johnny got dressed for the ride but when he came out the door Ray started laughing. Johnny had his dip net in one hand and a shotgun in the other. Ray kept laughing the whole time Johnny was walking to the boat.

What is that for?" Ray asked.

"Thought we might get a goose or two on the ride. Heard them fly over the other day. Might just get lucky," Johnny said.

"Might," Ray replied, "Might."

Johnny climbed in the little boat and off they went. It was a calm day on the water, just a slight chop. Johnny, in the bow, kept a close eye out for the black bobbing necks and heads of the geese. They were halfway between Norway, (the big island) and Sandy out in the middle of the lake when Johnny turned and looked at Ray. "Look! Look! Look!"

Johnny looked at Ray and then both men heard it.

"Don't look at me," Ray said. "Where are they?" Ray cut the motor to half speed. Johnny turned to see a flock of thirty or more geese flying fifteen feet above the water heading straight for them.

"Kill the motor," Johnny said, shaking his arm at Ray. But Ray had seen the geese at the same time and burped the throttle. The boat came to a rest. Forty yards out Johnny shouldered the twelve gage and touched it off. One goose hit the water. A quick reload and he took another shot at only twenty yards. The geese were going to fly right over them. Boom! One goose hit the water. One more quick reload and Boom! Johnny got off a third shot. A third goose spiraled into the lake. The flock scattered and gained height.

Johnny looked back. The second goose was laying on its back floating. The first goose was flailing around so he gave it a second round. Likewise, with the third goose. Johnny had taken a wing but it was trying to go. Boom! and it was floating. Supper was waiting.

Ray did a big "S" turn. Johnny with his dip net in hand, scooped up the geese one at a time. Three shots fired, three geese in the boat. Johnny was downright happy. Ray even more so.

"Well I think you might have a dinner for us," Ray said.

"Yessah," Johnny said as he dipped the last goose out of the lake.

The two men continued the trip across the lake reaching Sandy just before lunch. The short quarter mile hike to the lean to wouldn't take long. The two men gathered up everything Ray had brought. Most was already in his backpack but there was some loose things. Johnny tied most of the other items up inside a new wool blanket. With some fancy knot tying rope work he had his own pack to carry.

"One goose for dinner should be good," Johnny said to Ray. He picked one up out of the boat and the two men headed up over the ridge. When they reached the lean to, they could see that a bear had been by.

"Wasn't like this when I was here last," Ray said as he took off his pack. "Guess I'm going to have to change where I put things."

Ray held up the old wool blanket. It was torn to shreds.

"This was on the back wall."

Other things were moved around but there wasn't much there for the bear to mess with.

"Still want me to cook up the goose?" Johnny asked Ray as he held it up.

"Yea. I'm hungry and we will be here for a bit. Got to get things right. I'm going to use this place this fall," Ray answered.

The two men went to work. Johnny on the goose for dinner and Ray getting things, well, bear proof. Ray had brought some big spikes and he began building a stash box. Four-foot-long and three feet deep. Just a couple feet tall. This would give him all the room he needed. No longer would the blanket hang on the back wall of the lean to. Frying pan, coffee pot, caddie, even a little canned food would take its place. It still left plenty of room for odds and ends.

In no time Johnny had the fire going and set the rack off to the side so as not to overcook the goose. He added a couple of potatoes to a pot of water and sat this close to the fire so everything would be finished at the same time.

Meanwhile, Johnny had laid the goose out on its back and with his knife filleted the breast meat right off the bone. Two nice pieces of meat went on the rack.

"How are you doing Ray?" Johnny asked. "Your goose will cook in no time."

Ray laughed. "Just need to put a lid on it and it will be good."

Ray finished up just about the same time dinner was ready. The two men sat down to eat next to the fire pit using blocks of wood for seats. Johnny kind of sat with his back to Ray.

"I don't want to gross you out again Ray. Still making quite a mess when I eat.

"No problem," Ray said, "I understand." He felt sorry for the guy.

"Thought you weren't going to use this place anymore," Johnny asked while wiping his face.

"Well Busta did pretty good considering the hoof-ma-goof ate most of his catch. So, with him not around I figured I would take back over my line unless you had plans on it."

"No. I can't make it all the way back here. Not the way I am now," Johnny replied.

"That's what I figured, but I have a proposition for you. I will run the line, you do the skinning and stretching. We will split whatever comes off this line from here all the way back to your cabin. I will load the boat with traps and I will come over here. Then I will set them on the way over to your place and you will take my boat back. We can run it like that until the lake freezes."

"What about the bear?" Johnny asked.

"That three legged s.o.b.? I hope I see him again. My rifle will be in one hand or the other the whole time I'm up here. No damn hoof-ma-goof is going to scare me off my line." Ray's rifle was a .44 mag lever action. Not made for long shots but it will knock down anything in the Maine woods.

And so, it was set. Over the next couple of weeks Johnny helped Ray get ready for the trapping season. They put up some bait in Johnny's cabin so Ray's wife wouldn't have to deal with the smell. They boiled the traps and got them all waxed. Ray let Johnny take the boat back from Sandy while he hiked back to Johnny's cabin, remaking all of Busta's sets. Every cubby and pole set was remade and baited a couple weeks before the season started.

When the season was open Ray ran his other two lines first. He would let them sit for a couple of days before returning to check on them. Ray stopped by Johnny's to let him know to be ready at first light.

Chapter 12
Running the Line

Johnny was up a couple hours before daylight. He got dressed, made some coffee, and started the fire, then went outside to see what kind of day it was going to be on the water. It was cool with hardly any wind, just what he wanted. The ride to Sandy would be a good one and with weather like this he might even catch a fish on the way back home.

Johnny lit a candle and dropped it in to a mason jar then placed it on top of the big rock next to his landing. This was to signal to Ray that he was up and ready. He went back to the cabin, grabbed his fishing pole, net, and some small lures. He filled his thermos with coffee and put another log on the fire then closed the stove up so that he would have a good bed of coals when he returned. The door to the cabin was open and he could hear Ray's boat so with fishing pole in one hand and shotgun in the other, he headed to the beach. He set his stuff down by the rock and went back to close up the cabin and grab his pack.

Johnny reached the beach just as Ray shut the motor off. The boat banged and scraped against the rocky beach.

"Well look at you," Ray said.

"What?" Johnny asked, puzzled.

"Well I thought you would have all kinds of stuff with you but you just got that little pack. You all set to go?"

"Yup. Just need to blow out that candle." Johnny stepped out from behind the rock with gun, pole and net. Ray just laughed. "I knew it," he said, "I knew it."

Johnny added the gear to the boat then slid it off the beach. One final push then in he jumped. Ray started the motor then backed into deeper water. He dropped the motor down, put it in gear, and they were off. They just passed the big island as the sun broke the horizon. Mt. Katahdin was showing off all her beauty sporting a white crown of snow. A lot of leaves had lost their fall color and had already fallen. Winter was definitely on the way.

Steam rose off the lake as the men made their way to Sandy. It wasn't long before the ride was over.

"That wasn't too bad," Said Johnny.

"No. Couldn't ask for a better day," Ray replied as he climbed out of the boat. "Should see you back at your place this afternoon. Traps are in place. I just need to bait and set them. Shouldn't take long at all."

"You need help with anything at the lean to? Anything I can do for you there while you get going?"

"Nope. Just going to check on it and head out."

"Ok," Johnny said as he climbed back in the boat. "Have a good walk," he giggled, "See you this afternoon. And keep an eye out for that hoof-ma-goof."

"Good luck fishing. Or hunting. Or both," said Ray, smiling as he gave the boat a big shove back out into the lake.

Ray turned and headed up the trail to the lean to. Johnny got the motor started and pointed the little boat for the middle of the lake. The motor set at an idle would just putt along. Perfect speed for trolling. He rigged up the pole and let the line out. It would be a much slower trip back home. Johnny made two circles around the main part of the lake with no luck so he headed home. No geese either. Such a beautiful day and to have no fin or feather was a shame.

As he guided the little boat between the islands finally a fish had taken the line. A pickerel. It would be fish chowder for supper.

Ray was making his way, baiting and setting traps, back to camp, following Busta and his trap lines. It wasn't taking long at each set. Bait was missing here and there but that was a good thing. They were all done by critters and not the hoof-ma-goof. By the time Ray reached the beaver dam on Grant Brook he was wishing he had left a canoe there so he could paddle the rest of the way back to Johnny's camp.

It was late in the afternoon when he reached the cabin. The smell of fish chowder was lofting in the air. Ray gave a holler for Johnny who came running out of the camp.

"You okay, Ray?"

"Oh yea. Just a little tired. Forgot how long that trip was."

"Yea, I was thinking you would have been back by now," Johnny said.

"Things look good out there. A lot of bait missing and no sign of that dam bear either. Thinking of leaving a canoe over at Grant Brook though. Save me a little extra walking."

"Sounds like a good idea," Johnny replied. "I caught a nice pickerel on the way back. You want some chowder before you head back?"

"No, no thanks. It smells great, but if I don't eat at home with the wife, I'll be catching more than fur, if you know what I mean. Been gone all day. Gotta spend some time with the misses," Ray said, "I'll be back in a couple days. We will run her again."

"Ok," Johnny answered. He walked Ray down to his boat and helped him launch it. The wind had come up a little and there was a slight chop on the lake. Nothing Ray hadn't been out in before. Johnny couldn't help but feel winter was going to come soon.

The next day was cold and damp. Fog held close to the lake well into the morning. It only disappeared once the rain started. Johnny kept the fire going in the camp and thought to himself, it might not go out until springtime now.

Preparing for the days to come he sharpened his skinning and filleting knives then gave all the stretchers the once over. The fleshing board needed a little work. Busta hadn't done it any favors he thought as he sanded and worked out the nicks.

It was still raining slightly when Johnny made his last trip to the outhouse for the night. If it gets any colder there will be snow by morning, Johnny thought to himself. It will be a cold, wet ride across the lake, too.

At first light Johnny got the stove loaded back up. The camp had a chill to it, from all the rain he thought. He got the coffee ready and set it on the stove and waited for Ray. Opening up the door and stepping out on the porch Johnny saw why camp had a chill. It was snowing big, heavy flakes.

"Well this isn't good," Johnny muttered. You could only see fifty yards or so but out on the lake he could hear Ray's boat. He stood there listening and heard Ray go right by. He was too far out and couldn't see anything but snow. Johnny grabbed his boots and ran down to the lake.

"Ray!" he hollered. Ray couldn't hear him over the motor. "Ray!" he hollered again. Then he touched off his rifle. The motor went quiet. "Ray!" Johnny hollered once more.

"Yea!" Ray answered back.

"I'm over here," Johnny said, "You're going right by. Over here."

"Ok, I got ya."

Ray started the motor back up and turned the boat. Slowly a figure appeared on the lake. Out of the white snow came Ray. Ray started to laugh as Johnny came into his sight. The closer he got the more he laughed.

"What's so funny?" Johnny asked, "You were going right by."

"You cold?" Ray asked and started to laugh again. There Johnny was standing in nothing but a union suit. Hat on crooked and boots untied and rifle in hand.

"You're quite a sight this early in the morning," Ray said still laughing.

"Well now that you mention it, I am getting a little wet."

"Why don't we call it a day," Ray said, "You go get out of this weather and I will see you tomorrow. Fur should be moving in this boat but we don't need to be."

"Alright Ray. See you tomorrow," Johnny said as he waved and trolled back to camp. He stopped on the porch and listened. He could still hear Ray laughing. He went inside and got out of his wet clothes. The stove was going good and it didn't take him long to get warmed up.

The snow came down at a good clip for a few hours into the morning. By noon the sun was peeking through the clouds. Johnny was out stomping around in the fresh snow piling a little wood on the porch when Ray showed back up. Johnny waved as Ray landed his boat.

"Finally got some clothes on I see," Ray chuckled, "That was a sight, I must say."

"I don't know what was so funny," Johnny replied. Both men looked at each other and laughed.

"Thought we might take Busta's canoe up to the beaver dam on Grant Brook," Ray said. "Save me some walking time."

"Yea, sounds good," Johnny answered.

"The day turned out to be pretty nice," Ray said, "Thought we could get something done. Might as well check the traps at the dam at least."

"Yup, let's get that canoe," Johnny said.

As the two men took it off the wood pile and drug it down to the lake Ray noticed all the damage. Johnny looked at Ray and said, "Don't worry. It will still float. That bear did all this."

The look on Ray's face told Johnny he already knew that. They set the canoe in the lake, tied a long rope to the front of it and to the back then headed to the dam. As they motored by the big island, "Should have brought the pole Ray. This is where I got the pickerel the other day."

Not long after that they turned up into the brook. Ray raised the motor and slowed down, just putting up the brook. It was deep enough but you still had to go slow. They reached the spot where Busta had kept the canoe. With no problem, Johnny climbed out and held the boat while Ray made his way off.

"I'll take care of the canoe and stuff," Johnny said, "You go and check the traps." And with that Ray grabbed his pack and off he went. Johnny wasn't even out of sight when Ray gave a big whistle and a thumbs up. Johnny gave a big smile and a thumbs up back.

Once the canoe was tucked into the trees Johnny slowly made his way up to the dam following Ray's footsteps in the new snow. He kept looking around for Ray but he was nowhere in sight. He reached the dam and laying in the trail was a nice big beaver. Looking around more and following the footsteps, he could see Ray had already remade the set and moved on. Johnny rolled the beaver in the snow to get rid of extra water then tossed it on one shoulder and made his way back to the canoe. He waited for Ray to return wondering how far he would have gone. Johnny paced back and forth. Not even hearing a twig break, Ray stepped out in front of him jumping him. Johnny stumbled back and almost fell in the brook.

"What the hell!" he exclaimed. "You trying to give me a heart attack?"

"No but ain't the snow quiet to walk on."

"Yea, aren't you funny," Johnny replied.
Ray took off his pack. "Look what we got," he said as he pulled out a pine marten.

"Nice," replied Johnny. "I walked up and got that beaver. It's in the boat already."

"Good. Not a bad start. I see mink tracks up there by the dam. He'll find that set I made for him. Just going to take some time. I didn't go too far up the trail. Just the first couple of sets. This guy was just hanging around. No tracks to be seen but the snow stopped. I will run the rest tomorrow," Ray told him.

They hopped in the boat and headed back. The sun was low in the sky by the time they landed at Johnny's place. There was still plenty of light though to take care of that beaver so Johnny broke out his cradle and began skinning it right away.

"You want any of this for suppa Ray or for bait?"

"No, it's all yours Johnny but maybe some scraps for bait. Rib meat and stuff. You know, meat not guts," Ray replied.

"Ya, I hear you. We will drop what's left out in the lake on the ride tomorrow. I will save the casters for you too," Johnny said as Ray got in his boat and headed home.

"See you at first light," Ray said before firing up his little motor and setting for home.

Johnny finished skinning the beaver and quartered it up. The night was going to be cool so he hung up three of the quarters on the porch. The fourth was headed for the frying pan. Some of the beaver went in to mason jars, all the "good" stuff that Ray could use for bait. The rest Johnny laid down by the lake. He would be sure to get rid of it tomorrow.

Johnny took the martin up on the porch and hung it up then went in to fix some supper. Getting the wood stove going and heating up the cabin, potatoes, carrots, and onions went in to the pot. Then he cubed up the beaver and added that to the pot. Johnny let this sit on the stove and brew then went back to taking care of the pine marten. It would take a while for supper to be ready. Skinning, fleshing and stretching the little martin didn't take long so he broke out his fleshing board and knife. Johnny worked the beaver skin, inspecting every inch with every pass of the blade.

He had made hoops out of young birch after Ray and he had talked about trapping together. Johnny started lashing the beaver to the hoop, stretching it in to a circle; a little hole every inch or two all the way   around the hide threading with a piece of twine then around the hoop. Johnny did this all the way around the hide and then let it sit to dry.

After being on the stove for a couple hours the stew was ready. Johnny washed up and ate. A quick trip to the outhouse and back then Johnny filled the stove and went to bed.

The fire had died down and the cabin had cooled off when he woke up. He laid there for a minute just listening. He thought it was more than just the chill that had woke him. After a couple of minutes, he got up and filled his stove again checking the time. It was 2:30 in the morning. Well back to bed he thought. Ray wouldn't be there until 5:30 or 6:00.

Bang! Bang! Bang!

"Johnny, are you okay?" Ray hollered.

Johnny just about fell out of bed. "What? Huh?"

Ray opened the door. "Johnny, you okay?" he asked again.

"What the hell!" Johnny exclaimed as he grabbed his pants. "Yea, I must have fallen back asleep. I was up at 2:30, filled the stove and just laid back down. Guess I should have stayed up. Sorry. The water should be hot. Been on since 2:00 this morning," Johnny said while still getting dressed.

"Got these furs looking good," Ray said as he inspected the beaver. "How late did you work on him?"

"Not too late really. You want me to make coffee? Just need to get my boots and coat on."

"Yea. Water is hot you said. Shouldn't take too long," Ray replied and paused. "Never heard anything last night, huh?"

"That's the second time you asked that." Johnny turned and looked at Ray. "What's up?"

Ray opened the door back up and stepped aside. Johnny walked over and looked outside. There in the snow and all the way up on to the porch were bear tracks. Only three and a round impression where the fourth should have been. Johnny walked out stepping on to the porch. The

115

three quarters he had hung were gone. Looking towards the lake down to where he had left the carcass of the beaver was nothing but pink snow and tracks. Ray's boat sat not more than ten feet from it.

"I pulled up and thought the worst," Ray said.

"Well I am still here," Johnny replied as he walked back inside. Ray just looked at him. "Coffee?" he asked.

"Yea just a cup," Ray answered.

Johnny poured two cups of coffee and sat them on the table. Ray sat down and took a cup. Johnny walked over beside his bed and picked up his rifle then walked back to the table. He laid it down and picked up his cup. "Guess this will be coming with me," he said.

"Might be a good idea," Ray replied.

"I can't believe that bear is still coming around and I can't believe that I didn't wake up," Johnny said as he drank his coffee.

"Well ain't no one killed him yet. He's looking for all the free food he can get and he has got plenty this year. I just hope he leaves the line alone until we get some fur for ourselves," Ray replied. "I am about ready. You?"

"Yup." Johnny set his cup down, picked up his rifle, and headed out to the boat. Ray climbed in and Johnny launched the boat. It was a quiet ride over to Sandy. They reached the landing and Johnny hopped out holding the boat so Ray could come forward. He had his rifle in one hand and his pack in the other.

"Don't be wasting any time. Don't know about the weather today. And keep an eye out for that bear!" Johnny told Ray.

"The only thing going to slow me down is a pack full of fur," Ray said with a grin.

"I hope so. See you this afternoon."

"I should be back just about dark," Ray said as he turned and headed up the trail.

Johnny climbed back in the boat and headed back out on the lake and set for camp. When he arrived, he was a little nervous? He tried to be quiet in hopes of seeing the hoof ma goof and get a shot at him. After landing the boat and getting it tied off, he started to retrace the bears tracks in the snow. The tracks led him right behind the woodpile next to the outhouse where he had been the night of the fire. Johnny followed the tracks some more. The hoof-ma-goof was using the trail Busta had cut to the beaver dam up on Grant Brook. That was all Johnny had to see. Back to the cabin he went. He filled the stove and closed it up tight. After a quick change of clothes and a bite to eat Johnny got back in the boat.

Out on the lake he headed for Grant Brook, back to the beaver dam where they had been the day before. As he reached the stream, he idled down the motor and putted up the brook shutting it down just a little further down the brook where the canoe was. Johnny landed the boat and tied it off before making his way to the canoe. He would wait there until either Ray or the hoof-ma-goof showed up.

When he finally got to the canoe, he could see bear tracks right in their footprints. The hoof-ma-goof had passed within feet of the canoe but this time he left it alone. Slowly and quietly Johnny rolled the canoe over so he would have a dry place to sit. He settled in with his gun. It was going to be a long day.

The wind had picked up a bit but not enough to worry about getting back home. Johnny was enjoying the chickadees bouncing around in the birch trees just feet away. The sun was warming him even though the breeze had a chill to it now and again. Off in the distance a flock of geese were honking. Johnny listened to them as they grew closer and when they flew by at tree top level, he wished he had brought his shotgun. But he wasn't there for geese, he was there to make sure Ray got home.

The time flew by and the sun dropped on the ridge. Johnny knew someone would be arriving soon. Ray or the hoof-ma-goof? That was the question. As the sun touched the treetops Johnny was getting anxious, listening for the slightest sound. A branch broke on the other side of the brook. His heart rate jumped even though he never moved. Johnny was looking and listening intently but he could not see more than the edge of the trees.

"What are you doing here?" Ray asked.
Johnny jumped and almost fell in the canoe. "What the...how long have you been there?"

"Long enough to see you looking at the tree over there," Ray said. " Did it move? I thought you might shoot it," Ray giggled.

"Thought I heard something and you're not funny. One of these times you might just get shot. Can't be sneaking up on me," Johnny said. "I am going to tie bells to you so I can hear you coming." So, Ray asked again, "What are you doing here?"

"Well," Johnny began, "When I got back to camp, I followed those tracks that bear had left. They went right up the trail Busta had cut up to this dam. It comes out right over there."

As Johnny pointed the spot out something took off through the woods, breaking branches and pounding the ground.

"See, I told you I heard something! Let's get to the boat. It's down here."

"You want to take a couple of these?" Ray asked. "I got quite a load."

"What did you get? I didn't even see you carrying anything."

"Packs full. Left it up at the dam. Just bringing these 'coons to the canoe. Got another beaver up there too. I still need to take care of that set," Ray told him. "Leave them here. I will go get the boat and bring it up. Hot damn!" Johnny said as he turned around. "We got fur!"

Johnny went one way and Ray went the other. Johnny got the little boat started and idled up to the canoe. Ray took care of the beaver and remade the set. Looking up the pond he could see that the mink had made his rounds again that night and had found his way into Ray's trap. The sun was setting fast. Ray could hear Johnny load the boat as he remade the mink set. Looking back down toward the dam Johnny stood there with a thumbs up. Ray nodded and lifted the mink to show it off. Johnny went to grab the pack and Ray hollered, "Just grab that beaver. I'll be right down."

"Ok," Johnny said and did just that. He loaded the beaver in the boat then turned it so Ray could just step in back. It was only five minutes and Ray walked up. As he laid his pack in the boat he looked at Johnny and said: "I told you the only thing that was going to slow me down was a full pack."

Johnny looked down. Tails of all kind were hanging out of it.

"I'll be right back," Ray said and headed back to the dam.

"Where you going?" Johnny asked.

"To get the rest," Ray replied.

"What? More? How much more could you carry?"

"You'll see," Ray said as he disappeared behind a spruce tree. He came back with a coyote and a fox.

"I would never believe it if I hadn't seen it with my own eyes," Johnny said as Ray laid them in the boat and climbed in. Johnny hopped in the front and pushed them away from shore.

As Ray fired up the motor and headed down the brook to the lake, Johnny kept looking back at the load of fur Ray had been carrying. The moon was up and it was a good thing because it was dark when they landed the boat at Johnny's cabin.

"Everything goes in the cabin. That hoof-ma-goof ain't going to get any of this haul," Johnny said. He grabbed the two coon and went to grab the coyote, set it back down, and picked up the fox. "I still don't know how you carried all this."

Ray laughed and picked up his pack to throw it over one shoulder and reached down and grabbed the beaver by the base of the tail. In the corner of the cabin Johnny laid the coons and fox down then got the lantern lit. He went back for the coyote and when he came back in Ray had already emptied his pack. Three pine marten, two fishers, along with one weasel and the mink.

"Is there anything left on the line? Wow," Johnny said. "I mean wow. What didn't you catch?"

"Well," Ray began, "A cat (bobcat) and a rat (muskrat)." Both men started laughing. "I'd like to stay," said Ray, "but I'm sure the wife has suppa ready."

"Yeah, I got this. Tell her I said hi. You would be getting back real late if I hadn't been there with the boat."

"You know it. Would have been a long paddle after that haul. Thanks for being there. I'll see you tomorrow night maybe," Ray said as he left.

Johnny walked with Ray back to the boat. As Ray got in he said, "Keep that gun loaded. That bear is going to be back."

"I know, and it will be. I will be ready this time. He won't get up on the porch again without me knowing."

Ray idled the boat back out into the deeper water then headed for home. Johnny went back to the cabin. He started up the fire and stood there looking at the catch. He had a long day ahead of him tomorrow but food and a booby trap is what he was thinking about. After getting something to eat Johnny went about setting up his booby trap. Fishing line, two mason jars, an empty tin can and a big kettle. That surely would wake anyone up he thought. Fishing line tied to each then set on the edge of the roof with a main line running two feet off the floor at the top of the steps. That should do it.

After that Johnny went in and hung each animal up by twine so that they would be dry and ready for skinning in the morning. He realized that he and Ray hadn't talked about where each of them had come from or if he had seen any sign of the hoof-ma-goof. Right then it didn't matter. That fur was there and it was almost as much as Busta had gotten all season.

Johnny topped the stove off and went to bed. Rifle right beside him and lantern turned way down low. He would be sleeping light tonight.

He woke with a chill in the cabin and sun shining in the window. For as much as he thought he would see the crack of dawn he slept right through. He got up and raked the coals in the stove and got her going again. Looking out the frosted window he saw the sun was bouncing off the calm lake. Ice had formed all around the edge out to about ten feet or so. With the snow still on the ground and now ice starting on the lake winter wasn't but a few weeks away. Johnny put some coffee on and went to work making some breakfast. After he finished eating and putting the dishes away, he started on the fur. He took care of the martin first then the little mink, letting the morning chill come out of the air. One by one Johnny took the rest out front of the camp. Just off the porch he had a skinning pole all set up. The fox didn't take too long and neither did the coyote for its size. The coons and beaver would take him a while with skinning and fleshing to be done before being able to put on a board (stretcher). By the time all the fur was done it was midafternoon. Although it had warmed up some not much of the ice had melted from the shore and all the snow was still on the ground.

Time for some lunch he thought and just made it to the door when he heard Ray's little boat. He stopped and walked to the lake. As Johnny got to the shore Ray was ramming ice to land the boat.

"Didn't think I'd see you today," Johnny said.

"Well, I got up early and ran the other line with the truck. Didn't think you would want all them skun critters laying around with that hoof-ma-goof nearby."

"Well I just finished up. What do you want to do with them?" Johnny asked.

"Thought we might take them out to the big island. Throw them on shore for the eagles and crows. They got to eat too," Ray said.

"Sounds good. We need any of this beaver or coon for bait out on the line?" Johnny asked.

"Well, we could use a little. How about the legs of those marten and fisher?"

Johnny grabbed his hatchet and gathered up what Ray wanted while Ray loaded up the boat. Johnny got a little wet launching the boat with the ice and all but he made it in the boat and the men headed to the island.

The water was deep next to the island so Ray could keep the motor running as Johnny tossed the critters up on shore. After that they headed back to Johnny's place. Again, Ray crashed back through the ice in front of Johnny's.

"Coming in?" Johnny asked.

"For a minute," Ray said. "I want to see how that fur looks."

The two men headed for the cabin. Once inside Ray went right for the fur. Johnny dropped another log in the old wood stove. He stood watching Ray look over his work.

"Coffee, Ray?" Johnny asked.

"No thanks. Can't stay. Wife must have supper ready just about now." Ray paused. "Nice job with these Johnny. Nice job indeed."

"Thanks Ray," Johnny said smiling. "The coon and beaver need a little work yet. They need to rest a bit and let some of that oil come out. They will be fine in a day or so."

"Well I was thinking we would skip tomorrow then head out the day after. Hopefully we have another haul like this."

The men agreed and Ray left. Johnny went outside to clean up the mess on the ground, tossing it onto the fire pit by the lake. After that he filled his wood box before calling it a night.

Back inside he fixed himself some supper thinking he should have kept some of that beaver for himself. After eating and a trip to the outhouse, Johnny set up his trip wire "alarm" again just to be safe. "That damn ole hoof-ma-goof shows up I want to know about it!" he said to himself as he closed the door behind him. He checked the stove one last time and went off to bed.

When he woke the next morning, he could hear the wind blowing as he laid there in bed. He got up just long enough to load a few pieces of wood in the stove and peek outside. The lake was all white-caps. The ice that had formed around the shore was now just a pile on the rocky beach. Johnny slipped back into bed for a while.

The camp was nice and warm when he woke later. This time he got up and made coffee. Checking out the fur and sipping on his coffee, this would be the activity for the day, tweaking each hide as he saw fit. The wind got colder and colder as the day went on. When the wind did finally calm down just before dark it was well below freezing. Johnny knew tomorrow's trip to Sandy was going to be cold so he settled into bed early. Throughout the night he got up several times to add wood to the stove and look outside. With clouds in the sky he couldn't see more ice forming on the lake but he figured it would be there in the morning.

Johnny got out of bed before the sun rose. He filled the stove and put the coffee on. He wanted to be ready when Ray showed up. The sun was cracking through the skyline as he finished breakfast.

Johnny was headed for the outhouse when he heard Ray's boat motor come to life, breaking the still morning silence. Looking out on the lake he saw it was covered in a thin layer of ice.

Crash, crash, crash! The little boat was an ice breaker this morning. Johnny was dressed and already down by the lake when Ray got to his cabin.

"Cool this morning," Johnny remarked. "How much ice is out there?"

"Oh, half an inch or so! She's a little loud this morning!" Ray hollered.

"Yea I think they can hear you at Sandy," Johnny replied as he climbed in the boat.

Once out of the cove the ice was just a thin sheet and on the main lake it was non-existent. The outlet of Grant Brook was open they noticed as they went by. When they got to Sandy, they were breaking ice again. Ray crashed the boat onto shore.

"I'll meet you this afternoon at the same place," Johnny said.

"Sounds good," Ray replied. "Hopefully we have another good haul."

Ray headed up the trail and Johnny backed the boat out then headed for home. Today the trip seemed a lot longer. The cold breeze was cutting straight to the bone. By the time Johnny got back to his cabin his hands were numb. As he climbed out of the boat, he could see what was slowing him down. There was almost an inch of ice buildup on the front of the boat. The water was freezing to the rails and below all the way to the water line. Johnny tied off the boat then went and fetched a nice piece of firewood. With just a few whacks the ice popped right off. Then he went inside to warm up.

The stove had died down a bit but it was still plenty warm. He stood there for a minute rubbing his hands over the stove before adding more wood. He got out of his clothes and hung them to dry by the fire. The coffee was still warm so he fixed himself a cup then put on a new pot.

As the afternoon wore on Johnny got all dressed up again then set out in the boat to get Ray. The ice he had broken earlier that morning had refroze making it hard to get the boat turned around but after almost falling in a couple of times he managed to get it done. After using an oar to push himself into deeper water Johnny got the motor running and crashed through the ice. On his way all he could think about is how cold Ray would be and how much fur he would be carrying.

Johnny landed the boat and started a fire. He thought that he would be there a while but just a few minutes later Ray stepped over the beaver dam.

"Boy, you made good time today Ray."

"Easy to do with no fur. Hope you got a pot of coffee on at camp," Ray said as he walked by Johnny straight to the boat. He didn't say another word, just climbed in the boat. Johnny kicked the fire into the stream then untied the boat and jumped in. Ray fired up the little motor and held it wide open all the way to Johnny's cabin.

Inside Johnny poured Ray a cup of coffee. As he handed it to Ray, he asked, "No fur?"
Ray looked at him and Johnny could tell he was mad.

"Well," Ray began, "That dam hoof-ma-goof ate all the bait, all the sets, a coon and a martin. Sprung almost every trap."

"I would have thought he'd be sleeping by now," Johnny said.

"So, wouldn't I, but he isn't."

"This cold snap has got to put him out, wouldn't you think?" Johnny asked.

"That's what I kept thinking as I re-baited and remade the sets," Ray replied. He reached down in his pack and pulled out what was left of the martin and coon. Just the tails. "Oh yea, got one of these too,"

Then he pulled out a nice big pine marten. Johnny smiled.

"But that is the only one he didn't touch. Don't know why but don't care either. And if this cold keeps up, I will have to walk the whole line."

"You ain't going to make that trip in a day," Johnny told him.

"No. I will have to stay in the lean to. It is all stocked with wood, just have to bring a bed roll."

"I'll be making it with you," Johnny said.

"We'll see," said Ray. "Thanks for the coffee I want to get home before dark. I'm going to have to pull the boat up out of the water and get that motor off before it becomes part of the lake until spring."

Ray left and all Johnny could think of was that long walk all the way to the lean-to on Sandy. He hadn't tried walking that far for some time. Before the busted-up leg and the fire it wouldn't have been a problem but things were different now. All Johnny knew was he didn't want Ray doing it all by himself.

The next day it was still below freezing but the sun was out and there wasn't any wind. Johnny got up bright and early. He had one thing on his mind, to see if he could make it to Sandy and the lean-to. Johnny got all dressed up and started down the trail to the beaver dam. He figured if he could make it there and back and still had daylight then Sandy wouldn't be a problem.

Busta and Ray had blazed and marked a good trail. It was easy to follow but the little bit of snow was a drag. It was weighing down Johnny's bad leg. He had to stop every so often but he thought he was making good time figuring they had to stop at each set anyway. He could rest while Johnny was tending the sets.

Johnny reached the beaver dam on Grant Brook. There was ice on the pond but not enough to walk on yet so he headed back home feeling proud of making it in such good time.

The way back seemed a little easier. Walking in his own tracks his foot didn't drag as much in the snow. As long as he walked in Ray's tracks, he thought, he would be able to keep up. Even though it was cold out Johnny was breaking a sweat. His wool coat was unbuttoned and his hat was in his pocket. Switching hands, carrying the rifle that seemed to get heavier with each step. Each time he stopped to rest; the wait got longer before he started again. Only after he got cold would he head for home once again. By the time he could see the cabin Johnny was wiped out. The sun was low in the sky but he was back before dark. Cold and soaked with sweat Johnny stripped right down to his union suit as soon as he got in the cabin then wrapped himself in a wool blanket and stoked the wood stove. Once he was dry and warm, he fixed something to eat then loaded the stove and went to bed.

Chapter 13
Final Straw

Some time that night it began snowing big, fluffy flakes. By the time Johnny woke in the morning there was six inches on the ground. It was coming down good and hard so it was going to add up to even more.

Johnny, sore and stiff from the walk the day before, knew he would never be able to make the trip to Sandy in this kind of snow. He made coffee and got some breakfast but never dressed. He just sat around in his union suit. No one was going to visit him, not in this weather. He cleaned up the cabin a bit and tended to the last batch of fur, combing and wiping each one so he could get the best price.

Sometime around lunch the snow began to die down but it didn't look like it was going to stop any time soon. The coffee was working and Johnny had to head to the outhouse. No better timing with the weather. He stepped out with just his union suit and boots on. Sitting in the outhouse doing his business, he heard a noise and then another. It sounded like it was coming from inside the cabin but no one would be here. Not today. Not even Ray. Then, there it was again. Johnny hurried up and got out of the outhouse thinking someone was there or the cabin was on fire. He made his way to the door in a hurry. Johnny stopped dead in his tracks at the foot of the stairs. There in the fresh snow leading straight through the open door and from around the back side of the cabin were bear tracks. Three paw prints and one round circle pressed in the snow. The hoof-ma-goof was inside Johnny's cabin! With his rifle leaning against his bed all the way in back,

Johnny felt helpless. He turned to go back to the outhouse and hide until the bear left. The bear stepped into the open door and puffed at Johnny. It was only feet away and all that came to Johnny's head was run. He turned to go but instead of running to the outhouse he headed straight for the lake. The hoof-ma-goof bolted out of the cabin, bouncing off the door and frame. He jumped off the porch but lost his footing when he reached the ground. Johnny looked over his shoulder and watched as the bear tumbled over his heels. That gave Johnny just enough time to make it to the lake. The hoof-ma-goof kept coming so Johnny kept running. As soon as he hit the lake, he headed straight for Ray's house yelling at the top of his lungs. He hoped Ray was home and would hear his calls for help.

The ice was slippery under the snow and with only three legs the bear kept slipping. It slowed to a trot but was still coming after him. Johnny knew the path Ray had taken only a day and a half before with the boat and thought that ice wouldn't be safe. He tried to stay away from where the boat had been but when he heard the ice crack, he knew he was in trouble. Johnny froze, then turned and screamed at the bear. The hoof-ma-goof slowed to a walk. Johnny didn't dare to take a step. The ice kept cracking.

Boom! Boom! Johnny jumped and looked over his shoulder. Ray was running with his rifle, shooting in the air. He had heard Johnny's cry for help!

Johnny yelled, "The ice ain't safe! Stay back!"

"I know that you damn fool!" Ray hollered back. "Lay down so I can get a clear shot."

Johnny went to lay down but as soon as his knee touched the ice it broke free. Johnny disappeared. Ray dropped to one knee and fired at the bear. The hoof-ma-goof turned and ran back to the cabin. Ray stood there in disbelief waiting for Johnny to come back up. Ray waited and waited, and waited some more but Johnny was gone. Ray turned and went back to his house mad, angry, and saddened by what he had just seen. He looked up to see his wife in the window. She had watched the whole thing. Ray stomped the snow off his boots as he entered the house.

"I can't believe what I just saw," she said.

"Well believe it," Ray snapped. Johnny is gone and that bear is going to die today!

"What are you talking about? You can't go after him in this weather."

Ray walked right past her and started putting his gear together. Dry wool socks for starters, then wool pants over his union suit. A dry flannel shirt, his wool coat, hunting knife, rifle and fur hat. As he took his snowshoes off the wall, is wife asked him again not to go.

"That hoof-ma-goof has to die!" he said before giving her a kiss on the cheek and heading out.

He walked back down to the lake but before going back out on it he turned his little boat over, laid his gun and snowshoes inside and began pushing it across the cove. He was only twenty feet from the hole where Johnny had gone through when the ice finally cracked. Ray jumped in the boat not wanting to end up like his friend. He took out his oar and began pushing the boat with it. A little at a time he moved forward. He stopped and looked for any sign of Johnny when he reached the hole in the ice. Nothing to be seen but black water. Ray pushed the boat on. It took only a few more feet before the boat was back up on the ice.

With one foot in and one foot out Ray began pushing with his feet. When he got to where the hoof-ma-goof was standing he got out of the boat and searched for blood. Nothing was to be found but it was still snowing hard. The tracks were still there but filling in so Ray headed across the ice to Johnny's cabin. He was hoping the bear was still inside. Leaving the boat ashore Ray walked slowly to the open door of the cabin as he got closer, he could see the tracks went right by the outhouse and down the trail to the beaver dam on Grant Brook. Ray walked inside the cabin which was still warm even though the door had been open for some time. The hoof-ma-goof had made a mess again. As Ray looked around, he spotted the old oil lamp and Johnny's backpack. He grabbed both. He walked back down to the boat and picked up his snowshoes, went back to the cabin, and put them on. As he slid on Johnny's pack with the lantern inside, he said, "I'm going to get him Johnny. I'm going to get him or die trying."

The snow began to pick back up as Ray started down the trail. Ray figured the hoof-ma-goof was headed for his den and he didn't want to have to climb inside to get him, so at a fast pace he followed the tracks down the trail. The wind hadn't picked up but the snow had. It was coming down hard, slowly filling in the tracks that he was following. By the time he reached the beaver dam the sun had set and darkness was coming. Ray had gained on the bear. The hoof-ma-goof had no fear and no idea he was being followed. He was taking his time heading to his den to sleep for the winter but Ray had other plans.

Ray followed the tracks across the dam and back into the woods. The hoof-ma-goof seemed to be following the trap line. The wind had picked up a bit and the snow at times was almost a white-out. The tracks in the snow were fading, all but the round stump. It didn't stay on top or fill in like the other three footprints. Every three or four feet there was a hole in the snow.

At one point it had gotten dark enough that Ray had to light the lantern. He had a hard time with the wind and snow but with the light Ray could follow the holes in the snow. The trap line looked a lot different at night, especially in a snowstorm. Every once in a while, Ray would see something and think he knew where he was but he wasn't sure. He never left the tracks though.

It was late in the night when Ray had caught up with the hoof-ma-goof. The tracks were fresh and Ray could see all of them. He knew he wasn't far behind. The snow hadn't let up and neither had the wind. Snow falling from the trees made it impossible to see more than a few feet. The light from the lantern bounced back off everything white almost blinding Ray at times. He knew the hoof-ma-goof would be able to see him long before Ray could see him but he needed to keep following him or risk losing him. Looking down the tracks, Ray noticed something was different. He was looking at snowshoe tracks. The hoof-ma-goof had circled.

Ray took the lantern and raised as high in the air as he could looking under the light. The wind swirled around then Ray heard something different. That wasn't just the wind. The snow fell out of the tree branches right in front of Ray blinding him in a wall of white. As it faded Ray could see something but couldn't make it out. The moment he realized it was the hoof-ma-goof standing on its hind legs looking him straight in the face it was too late. Ray dropped the lantern and started to raise his rifle but the hoof-ma-goof dropped and charged. Ray went to step back but with the snowshoes on he fell on his back. Just as he hit the ground the hoof-ma-goof was at his feet. Ray fired his rifle and the hoof-ma-goof landed on top of him. One lucky shot right through the Adam's apple broke the bears spine, killing him instantly.

Ray laid there a minute trying to figure out what had just happened then he tried to move. His ankle was sprained and collar bone broke but he was alive...for now. The hoof-ma-goof had landed on him and the lantern staving Ray up and putting out the lantern. Ray was in no shape to build a shelter or crawl and get wood for a fire but he needed to stay warm for the night or risk freezing to death. He took out his knife and slit the belly of the bear. He rolled out the guts and slid in as far as he could. He passed out from pain and exhaustion.

Three inches of snow covered the bear and Ray's legs were cold when he woke. To him that was a good sign. It meant they weren't froze. Moving slowly, Ray got up and got his bearings. The sun was coming up and so was the temperature. Looking around Ray realized that he was only a hundred yards from the lean-to on Sandy Stream. He couldn't believe it. Limping on his snowshoes, Ray made his way there with his rifle and now broken lantern in hand. The lantern still had some oil in it and Ray knew there was plenty of wood there.

Once at the lean-to Ray got a fire going, a big fire. He threw boughs of fresh cider, spruce and hemlock on it to send up a plume of smoke big enough for his wife to see across the lake. She had gone next door after Ray left and told her neighbor what had happened to Johnny and how Ray had gone after the bear. Kermit and his wife assured her that Ray would be alright and if he wasn't back that night then Kermit would go find him. So as soon as she saw the smoke, she knew it was Ray. When she reached Kermit's front door she didn't even get to knock. Kermit opened the door.

"I see the smoke. That has to be Ray. No one would be over there. I think that is coming from his lean-to. It's over that way somewhere. I will find him," he told her. "Look for smoke just before dark. If it is in the same place it means I am with him and we will be home tomorrow. If you don't see it we are close to home."

Kermit didn't take any chances. He had a small pack of food and supplies for the night's stay. He went out and hopped in his truck and drove around the cove then took the path Busta had cut to camp from the main road. He made it to the cabin and saw the mess the hoof-ma-goof had left. He quickly started a fire just in case they got back soon, then he headed down the trail.

There was hardly a trace of where Ray had gone but if he stepped off the trail a little bit, he'd sink a little more in the snow. That's all he needed to help guide him. When Kermit finally reached the beaver dam on Grant Brook, he decided to walk to the lake just to see if there was still smoke on the ridge. It was only a couple hundred yards down the brook. As he made his way out of the woods and on to the lake Kermit could still see smoke rising. A big puff would come up through the trees then it would slow, followed by another big puff. Somebody was feeding that fire. Kermit was betting it was Ray.

The edge of the lake was frozen all the way around as far as Kermit could see so he decided to walk to shore rather than go through the woods. Within the hour Kermit had made his way over to Sandy, keeping an eye on the smoke the whole time. Before Kermit set back in the woods, he hollered for Ray but got no response so he touched off his rifle. Ba-boom! It echoed across the lake. An answer came back with another ba-boom coming from the direction of the smoke. Kermit started up the ridge but had no trail to follow, just a bearing on his compass in the general direction of the smoke. He was half way up over the ridge when he could smell the smoke. He pulled the trigger of his rifle again, then jumped when a shot rang out close to him.

"Ray!"

"Over here!" he replied. Kermit changed course and in just minutes was standing with Ray.

"You're a sight for sore eyes," Ray said as Kermit stepped out into the open.

"Your wife is worried something awful about you," Kermit told him. "You spent the night here? You okay? You look like crap."

"Thanks," Ray said. "You must be ready for some coffee. That was a long walk. What time did you leave?" Ray tossed Kermit a cup and pointed to the coffee pot sitting next to the fire.

"I figured somebody would come if I put up enough smoke," Ray said.

"Well I think I left about half an hour after I saw the smoke," Kermit replied.

"She tell you about Johnny?" Ray asked.

"Yeah she did."

"Well to answer your questions," Ray said, looking at Kermit. "No. I'm not okay. I think my collarbone is broke. Can't use my left arm very well and my ankle is messed up but I can walk."

"What happened?" Kermit asked him.

"Well that damn bear fell on me. I couldn't move and I didn't know where I was so I gutted him out and slept inside the stinky s.o.b."

"You did what? You're kidding me, right?"

"Nope," Ray answered. "He is right over that hill. I am going to need your help skinning him and getting the meet back home."

After a few minutes of finishing their coffee and letting the fire die down, the two men made their way up over the hill where they had come upon the aftermath from the night before. Kermit couldn't believe his eyes. The snow told the whole story. Kermit went to work skinning the hoof-ma-goof making sure to leave the paws on the hide so he could show the people in town the bear was dead. Kermit made a drag for Ray and they tied it to his belt since he couldn't wear his pack but they had a bear hide and plenty of meat to pack out. Making their way for home by way of the shoreline the two men walked as the sun set and the moon rose. They only left the shoreline to cross the beaver dam and avoid thin ice, then back down to the lake. It was well into the evening when they reached home.

The word spread about how Johnny died and how his friend had gone after the bear that chased him out onto that thin ice. The head of the hoof-ma-goof was mounted and hung on the wall at the Big Moose Inn so everyone would remember Johnny Blueberry and the hoof-ma-goof.

The bartender just looked at me for a moment then said, "So Johnny died. The bear died. Busta skipped town and Ray shot the bear and that bear's head is hanging out in our entryway?"

"Yup. That's the hoof-ma-goof," I told her.

"So why haven't I ever heard this story before? I've worked here for twenty years."

"Well, you weren't here when I was ten," I replied with a smile.

Dedication

I need to thank James Mcquarrie, (my friend), for stopping and taking me along that night, and to the man that told the story of the Hoof-ma-goof that night, I will never forget it.

This is the story of a bear that tormented Millinocket Lake and the surrounding area in the 1900's, and three of the men, Busta, Johnny and Ray, that had encounters with the hoof-ma-goof.